I0573381

Stone House Farm

Rhobin Lee Courtright

A Wings ePress, Inc.
Romance Novel

Wings ePress, Inc.

Edited by: Jeanne Smith
Copy Edited by: Christie Kraemer
Executive Editor: Jeanne Smith
Cover Artist: Rhobin Courtright

All rights reserved

Wings ePress Books
www.wingsepress.com

Published In the United States Of America

Wings ePress Inc.
3000 N. Rock Road
Newton, KS 67114

Dedication

To Jan, with whom I share so much.

***

One

Manistee, Michigan, 2009

Claws of anger ripped Amanda Blanchard's chest as she read the legalese of the document she held. Jaw clenched, she slid the papers back into the envelope and jammed it into her purse. She would not accept anyone threatening her home. Grabbing her coat, she thrust her arms into the sleeves as she walked through the office, telling Nan, "I'll be back in half an hour."

Nan glanced up and nodded her gray-haired head to indicate she heard, but never stopped writing as she spoke into the phone. Nan acted as office manager and receptionist, although she and her husband owned Olson Bookkeeping. More important to Amanda, they had supported her not only financially with her job, but also emotionally through the past few years of personal turmoil.

Outside, the frigid air failed to cool her rage and the gray sky promised another deluge of icy rain, making the yellow and purple crocus lining the sidewalk look unnaturally bright. Piles of winter's snow plowed from the parking lot lined the pavement's edges; most mounds towered over the cars. She backed her old Taurus out of its parking place and turned onto Highway 31 where, in recent years, a corridor of stores and offices had grown along the road leading into Manistee.

Five minutes later, she parked her car on River Street in front of a remodeled nineteenth-century store that housed the prestigious Preston Development Company. The conversion from store to office building had been beautifully executed while keeping the structure's historical style. The sight only inflamed her more, reminding her of whose history was at stake.

She pushed through the glass front door expecting to have to plow past secretaries and assorted office henchmen, but as luck would have it, Wade Preston stood in the reception area talking with his partner, Edward Van Haitsma. Wade's height and dark hair made a strong contrast to his partner's shorter frame and fair hair. Both were good looking by anyone's standard. Wade held a stack of papers. The two men looked as if they had just finished a heated discussion.

"Whatever you want!" Van Haitsma said as he turned and walked away, his shoes pounding an upset rhythm on the polished oak flooring.

Preston's fiancée, Melissa Rillema, stood nearby with her arms crossed. A pout marred the perfection of her face. Since only the woman's mouth moved, without a hint of frown lines, Amanda snorted, suspecting cosmetic injections. Melissa would make a perfect wife for Wade. Two beautiful, congenial rich rats running in a social superiority maze. Melissa's long blonde hair rippled about her shoulders as she turned her head to glance at Amanda, then back to Wade, who had walked over to Melissa.

As Amanda strode forward to interrupt the couple's private interlude, Wade looked over at her, anger etching his face. She checked her step before charging ahead. Hell, he had to expect a storm after the letter he had sent her. As Wade watched her approach, his face firmed into what Amanda privately called the 'bulldog behind the businessman's mask.' It infuriated her to have to spend her precious lunchtime taking care of this matter. This time, she would talk to Wade Preston face-to-face and make her position clear.

"Mrs. Carter, how can I help you?"

He recognized her? His voice and demeanor were politely bland, but remnants of anger lingered in lines around his handsome features. He had called her by her married name, something she had discarded after her divorce.

She held Preston's gaze with determination. As a freshman teenager in high school, with hormones and the idealism of innocence, Amanda's dream world starred the senior quarterback, Wade Preston. Back then, he had been oblivious of her.

"It's Ms. Blanchard, now. You can help me, Mr. Preston, by accepting the fact that I do not want to sell my property. Not now, and not in the future. Furthermore, I will not let you steal it from me." Heads turned toward the sound of her angry tones. Most looked like employees and quickly looked away when Amanda stared back at them. Wade's face deepened in color, his mouth and jaw set, his eyes darkening.

She waved the envelope under his nose. He took it, looked at the address, and pulled the sheets from inside. His brows scrunched lower as he read.

"You've received an offer at a fair-market price," Wade said, his voice firm, low and controlled. Her temper eased slightly seeing the wrinkle between his brows as he looked at the letter.

Melissa smiled pityingly at Amanda. "I would think in your dire circumstances, Wade's offer was manna from Heaven." Her tone held pure condescension.

"Stay out of this," Wade said with a fierce gaze at his fiancée. Amanda thought Melissa's smile more smirk than compliance and doubted the woman had even heard her lover.

"What could you possibly know about my situation?" Amanda said. "And how does any of this involve you?"

The smile never faltered. "I understand it is a very generous offer."

Amanda's rage fired anew. Melissa had no part in this, and her opinion was not only unneeded but also unwanted. "Generous if I were willing to sell out what my family worked generations to build.

I'm not." Amanda turned back to Wade Preston, grabbed the letter from his hand, and clutched it in her fist.

His frowning gaze turned to Amanda, his brows lowering until they nearly touched. "I don't know what you are alleging. As I said, this is an offer at a fair market price for your property."

"You missed the threat of an eminent domain seizure. I don't care what dirty tricks you try with the bank, or the county planning department, or the commissioners, or the township board. I will fight you every step of the way."

"Then you'd better hire a lawyer." Melissa cut in with a practiced tinkling sound that substituted for a laugh.

"Melissa..." Wade's tone held a warning and his scowl deepened.

Amanda kept her regard on Wade, hoping her expression said 'I am not backing down.' If not pumped with so much adrenaline, she would never have felt so defiant, but Melissa's confidence ate at her self-assurance. Her diffident side advised retreat. Having said what she wanted, she turned on her heel and swept out of the office, escaping any further humiliation.

~ * ~

Amanda pulled her car into a parking space in the small strip mall housing Olson Bookkeeping. Fearlessness abandoned her as her anger eased. Reality loomed. She could not afford a lawyer. Wade Preston knew that. He probably had her background checked and knew how the divorce settlement had affected her. She was going to lose her home, fail her heritage.

Stop feeling sorry for yourself and move! There must be an answer to this problem.

Taking a deep breath, she pulled the latch on the door and left the car. Work called. She had to balance the books for two clients before she could begin preparing their tax reports, and she had to do it today. Once in her office, Amanda could not settle down to the tasks she needed to complete. After losing her concentration yet again, she picked up the phone and dialed the only person who would commiserate.

"Lark? Hi, it's me."

"Hi, Mandy," Lark answered, her voice filled with her joyful exuberance for life.

"Knew you'd be home today."

After a second's silence, her perkiness gone, Lark asked, "What's wrong?"

"Preston Development Company has made an offer to buy my land. Preston's already got all the northern parcels surrounding my acreage. His partner, Edward Van Haitsma, received a variance on the land from the county, and there are plans to put a new road in that will cut my farm in half. What am I going to do?"

"For crying out loud, Amanda. Go to the commissioners' meeting. If you want your land, fight for it."

Amanda took a breath that broke on a sob. "I doubt they will listen to me. I have winter taxes outstanding."

~ * ~

The temperature steadily dropped through the afternoon. Rain pelted her office window in freezing drops. Amanda turned on the local radio station and listened when a deep voice relayed a severe weather warning. She sighed, knowing how the lake-effect could worsen the approaching storm. The news announcer repeated the warning every ten minutes, advising drivers to get home and, if possible, stay off the roads.

When she left her office, the rain had stopped. Dark, bare oak and maple branches lined the bottom edge of a lead-colored sky. She read the promised snow in the atmosphere. Already, a few large snowflakes glided in feathery, whirling motions through the air. With the predicted bad weather, she had canceled several appointments for tomorrow. She mentally ran through a checklist of jobs needing completion. As much as she might want to avoid the issue, her thoughts returned to Wade Preston. Anger from her noon encounter and pessimism sapped her spirit, which seemed to match the late afternoon gloom.

Amanda watched the threatening sky as she drove to pick her daughter up from preschool. Groceries already lined the backseat of the old Taurus. She and Kari would be home long before the forecasted weather hit in full fury. Pulling the car into the Wee Care Daycare

Center, Amanda pulled her unbuttoned coat around her and ducked into the building.

"Mommy!" Kari shouted and ran for a hug as Amanda entered the door into the preschoolers' room off the main entrance. Kari's resemblance and enthusiastic greeting always reminded Amanda of Marla, her cousin and Kari's birth mother. Marla had passed away too early in life. Amanda scooped Kari up and gave her a quick hug and kiss. "Have you been good today?"

Kari nodded, wisps of dark hair escaping from her braid, giving her adopted daughter a wild, elfin look. Amanda smiled as Kari confessed, "Pretty good."

She gently rubbed at a smudge on Kari's cheek. It didn't come off and Kari flinched.

"It's a bruise," Kari's teacher Kay said. "Jimmy Patrick hit her with a toy." She held Kari's coat. "But it was a play accident. She walked up behind him as he pulled a block out of where it was stuck in another toy. His flailing arm caught her."

Amanda inspected the bruise. "You okay?"

Kari nodded. "He didn't mean to do it. He said he was sorry."

Kay and Amanda talked a few minutes longer while Amanda helped Kari put on her coat. When they were ready to go, Kay asked, "How are the roads?"

"Not bad, yet. A typical Michigan April."

"Unpredictable? The weather is all anyone is talking about." Kay laughed again and held the door for Amanda and Kari to leave. "Be careful!"

Amanda smiled back at Kay and waved. With Kari strapped in, she backed the car out and started the drive home. The day's rain mixed with snow made the roads slushy, and Amanda watched for icy patches, leaving plenty of space between her Taurus and the other vehicles on the roads. She had once wanted all types of adventure, both physical and romantic: trips to Europe, Australia, China, even the Antarctic. She had dreamed of men who drove her to dizzy heights of rapture.

Since Grant Carter, though, she only wanted safety.

When she reached the country road where it left the busy highway, she felt more secure. The road was easy to traverse; the puddles lightly skimmed with ice still held good traction at their base. Turning into the long drive up to the old farmhouse, she felt a sense of relief even though her home looked dark in the gloomy weather. Wetness darkened the mélange of the silver and brown rocks of its construction. Arched stone piers held up the front porch roof. While of the Victorian era, the structure's clean straight lines gave the design a timeless quality. A side porch, invisible from this angle, and added many years ago, existed on the far side. Her grandma had always referred to it as the drying porch. The barn's foundation and the old silo were also constructed of fieldstone. Several years earlier, a magazine had featured the house and barn in an article on Midwestern stone houses. Her father had been alive then. Amanda felt an ephemeral warmth surround her heart as she gazed at her house. She would not relinquish it without a fight.

She drove the car into the detached garage near the barn as snow began to fall in a heavy curtain. Unstrapping Kari from her car seat, Amanda hurried her into the house. It took another three trips to lug in grocery bags.

Stew cooked in the crock-pot sitting on the kitchen counter next to the old sink. The scent filled the air. Amanda sighed in contentment at her morning forethought while she toasted some cornbread made a few days earlier. It took only a minute to place two dishes of stew and bread on the table. Filling a glass of water for herself, and milk for Kari, they sat down to dinner.

She let Kari finish eating while she put the groceries away, lit a fire in the ancient cookstove for extra warmth, and made four trips to bring wood for the fire into the house.

As she emptied the contents of the last grocery bag, Amanda heard a bang and looked out the small window over the sink. One side of the barn's double doors stood open. As she watched, the wind blew it shut. The plank door slammed shut to bounce open with enough force to bang against the barn walls again.

"Damn." Had Tina not fastened the old latch tight when she left? She had to go out and close it, so she might as well check Noona now and make sure she was bedded properly. Noona's foal might well save all of them. "Kari, I need to go to the barn. Have you finished your supper?" Amanda looked at her daughter and grabbed a towel to clean her up. "Do you want to go along?"

"All done, don't want to go outdoors."

"Then play in the living room while I see to Noona." She followed Kari into the living room, uttering a string of dos and don'ts. She worried about leaving Kari alone, even for a few minutes.

"Turn on the TV," Kari ordered.

Amanda did and inserted Kari's favorite animated feature into the DVD, the last appliance purchase Amanda had made at a garage sale—six years ago. "All right, you stay right here. When I get back, I'll read you a story, so pick one out, okay?"

"Okay." Kari was already engrossed in the beginning of the movie.

As Amanda slipped into her barn boots and a heavy jacket, her thoughts ran wild with guilt. When in an unhappy marriage, raising a child alone had seemed preferable. Reality differed. Before Grant took off, Amanda knew her marriage had been impossible, but she would have remained, endured—after all, for better or worse. Grant chose differently. He had simply emptied their joint bank account and filed for divorce, demanding half the acreage belonging to her family's centennial farm. In the end, he did not get all he wanted, but she had to give him forty acres, sell some heirloom jewelry, and all but one of her prize horses to finalize the divorce. Afterward, he left.

Tina's gelding stuck his nose out over his stall door as she entered, but Noona's stall stood empty. Not good! The foal due in a few weeks came from money scraped together to have the mare bred. Noona was the last of her father's prized Morgans.

She could do nothing now. Later, when Kari was in bed and asleep, she would find Noona. Maybe the dratted mare would return. Meanwhile, Amanda released Buck from his kennel. The dog had received his size and color from his black lab father, and his coat length from his retriever mother. Buck romped and rolled in the thin layer of snow already lining the ground.

"Settle down," Amanda commanded as he rushed through the back door ahead of her. He brought cold air and an overzealous tail into the kitchen. Plopping onto the bench next to the back door, she pulled off her boots and hung up her coat.

Swiping a strand of hair from her face, Amanda made sure the dog had food and water. Kari remained engrossed in her video. Amanda sat to watch with her, and Kari crawled onto her lap. Once the movie ended, it would be time for her bath and bed. The nighttime ritual was always the same: bath, room pickup if needed, tucking in, and a story. Once she was sure Kari slept, Amanda found a flashlight, dressed for warmth, and went to search for Noona.

"Come on, Buck." She let the whining dog out the door. Outside, a stiff wind blew, thick with snow. Buck bounded away. It was dark out, the sky invisible. Walking became a slow process. The snow fell steadily, obscuring the view of the surrounding land. Even with a strong-beamed flashlight and utter familiarity with the terrain, the trek still seemed a little scary. Snow already lined the tree limbs. Drifts smoothed the uneven ground in unexpected pockets of foot-devouring snow. Although dressed against the cold, Amanda could feel the temperature's change from a few hours earlier. The storm seemed to promise all the television and radio reports predicted, and perhaps more. She had listened to the report and then turned the television off to put Kari to bed. Leaving Kari alone in the house while she searched for Noona lashed her with guilt.

She walked the fence-lined track between two orchards that led to the pasture on the back acreage. Amanda stopped every few minutes and checked the way, trying to locate Noona. No hoof tracks marred the pristine whiteness, but at the end of the path, Amanda saw the gate had blown shut. Noona stood, head over the top rail, nickering in welcome. Amanda walked up and placed a lead line on the mare's halter before opening the gate. Sides bulging with her pregnancy, Noona did not look distressed or about to go into labor. The mare wore a blanket and Amanda checked the straps.

"Naughty girl!" she said softly, starting to lead the mare back to the barn. She stopped, realizing Buck was not with her. "Buck! Here, Buck. Come, Buck!" When only silence answered her, she called again and heard a faint bark. Repeated calls brought more barking, but no Buck. "You see where your truancy got us?" Amanda asked the mare. "He's probably caught his collar on some shrub." She tied the lead to the fence before she climbed over the slippery rails into the northern orchard to find what had distracted Buck.

By concentrating on the direction of the now constant barking, she searched. When he fell silent, she would call and the barking would resume. The orchard looked unfamiliar in darkness and falling snow, with tree limbs appearing to loom out of nowhere and the ground strangely transformed. With frequent calls, answered by Buck's barks, she homed in on the dog. He looked like a dancing shadow in the surrounding whiteness.

His collar had not trapped Buck. An unusual long mound of snow lay under one of the apple trees. The dog barked and dug around the shape. Approaching with caution, Amanda swept her flashlight's beam over the mound and caught a flash of khaki and fingers. The mound was human. She hurried her steps. Kneeling, she rolled the camouflage-jacketed form over. His face was pale and drawn; his black hair ice-coated and dark, wet strands plastered his forehead. Wade Preston!

"What are you doing out here? Visualizing where to put your condominiums and golf course?" she asked the unconscious face. He had to have walked there. She noticed shallow snow-filled footprint impressions in the snow. Why come now, during a snowstorm?

"This makes as much sense as anything has lately," she complained to Buck.

Buck whined, his tail striking her back as he stuck his head under her arm and snuffled the coat of the prone man. She pushed Buck away. "Good-boy, yes, you found him, down."

She pulled off her glove and felt his face. Wade was cold, too cold, his lips blue, his skin deathly pale.

"Please, God, don't let him be dead," she whispered, feeling his throat for a pulse. She found a beat and sighed in relief. Taking off her jacket, she threw it over him. Jumping up, she ran to Noona, climbed the fence, and slid onto Noona's back before untying the lead.

It was dangerous, but she pushed Noona into a gallop back to the barn. Once there, Amanda jumped off the mare, led her into her stall, and latched it. She grabbed the slick piece of plastic Kari used as a sled and some old horse blankets and ran back the way she had ridden. Several times her feet slipped, forcing her to catch her balance and slowing her progress as she moved through the rapidly accumulating snow. She arrived out of breath. Falling to her knees, she pushed and pulled him onto the sled, calling, "Wade, wake up. Wade!" Wade's eyelids flickered, but he didn't respond.

Amanda continued shouting, unable to stop, though she doubted he heard as she pulled his body. His eyelids fluttered and opened. He raised his head. His gaze locked on her.

"You!" His soft, hoarse outcry cost him; his head fell back and his eyes closed to mere slits. He gasped as she pushed him onto the sled, his face grimacing, his eyelids scrunched shut.

"Why not me? You're trespassing on my property."

Wade's words came thick and slow. "Is that why you shot me?"

Two

"Shot you?" Shock crackled in Amanda's voice. "I didn't shoot you!"

He never responded. His eyes closed, and the grimace smoothed from his features, showing he had passed out. She shivered both from cold and from Wade's accusation. Shot! Someone had shot him? She flashed the light over the depression his body had left in the snow, saw bloodstains, but the only footprints were hers and his.

Frightened, she scoured the landscape looking for any intruder. Only the snow-crusted trunks of apple trees appeared. Their regular spacing seemed somehow menacing as they blurred into the blowing snow and the darkness beyond the short beam of light.

No one's here but me, and Wade needs help now.

She put her coat back on and threw the blankets over Wade. She tucked the edges under him, wrapping her scarf around his head. Pulling the sled back to the house seemed to take forever, though it floated easily over the snow despite Wade's legs hanging over the back end, dragging two furrows in their trail. He weighed a lot more than Kari did.

The snow fell heavier. Only the light on the back door provided direction. Buck bounced along next to her, leaping through already accumulating drifts.

She struggled to pull Wade's weight onto the back porch, slipped, and fell twice, swearing. Finally, she managed to maneuver his body through the back door, her breath heaving. After closing and locking the door, she collapsed on one of the three steps up into the kitchen. She glanced at Wade. "Thank heaven. It's probably a good thing you aren't aware of how badly I'm manhandling you." Catching her breath, she pulled off her coat, and threw it on one of the pegs on the wall. Amanda pushed his torso into a sitting position, wrapped her arms under his shoulders, and clasped her hands over his chest. Grunting, she dragged him up the three steps from the landing into the kitchen.

Leaving him on the wood floor, she rushed to the phone. The line was dead. She tried dialing 911 twice, but it was a useless gesture. "Damn, I need to get a cell phone." Ice must have brought the line down, she reasoned. She could not call for help, and if there were someone out there...had someone really attacked Wade? She glanced at his unconscious form on the floor, recalling the blood. "Hunting season is over. Someone purposely shot you?" Fighting panic, she raced upstairs. Kari slept in angelic peace. Leaving her daughter, she ran through the house turning off lights, locking the back door, pulling down window shades, and shutting curtains.

In dread, Amanda returned to look at the unconscious man on her kitchen floor. *I cannot get him help. What am I to do?* She looked at the storm raging outside her kitchen windows. Anyone out there might see the kitchen light. She stepped over Wade, pulled down the shades, and closed the curtains she had overlooked.

Buck's nails clicked on the floor as he paced the room to his basket by the stove. He curled into the basket and watched Amanda, his tail giving a few thumps on the floor. Surely, he would bark if anyone came near the house. Her attention returned to Wade.

"Ninny!" she admonished herself. "Do what you can." She retrieved logs from the woodpile outside, carefully locking the back door before stoking up the fire in the wood-burning cookstove.

She dashed upstairs for supplies. Band-Aids, small gauze pads, and a few tubes of various ointments filled a basket in a bathroom drawer. Under a basket, the edge of a book peeked out. Her first-aid book. Grabbing it, she ran to the linen closet and pulled out sheets and extra blankets. Another quick check showed Kari's chest rising in the smooth rhythm of sleep. Amanda ran back downstairs, taking the steps two at a time.

Wade had not moved. She tried the phone again. Silence. Picking up the first-aid book, she looked up what she needed to know.

"Find out where and how badly the victim is injured." Talking as she read helped clear her mind. "The injured being the latest man to make my life miserable, but that is unimportant right now."

The skin on his ashen-gray face was too cold. The room was warm, though, almost too warm, the old stove doing its work nicely. She unzipped his parka. Blood soaked the inside and smeared on her hands as she removed it. Blood also soaked his shirt. She cut it off with scissors retrieved from her sewing kit.

A raw wound seeped blood at the top point of his left shoulder, disfiguring the smooth contours of a muscular outline. Whatever wounded him seemed to have passed through his body. *Had a bullet caused this? Had someone really shot him? Tried to kill him?*

As she asked herself the question, a sinking feeling curdled in her stomach. He had accused her of shooting him, and the wound certainly looked like that.

His skin felt icy cold. Hypothermia, she guessed, a condition as deadly as a gunshot wound. She picked up the book. "The victim must be warmed quickly. Remove any wet clothing and wrap the victim in blankets,'" she read aloud. "What about the bleeding? Bandage first or warm first? This is no help." She threw the book down and took a deep breath.

She quickly cut up a sheet and formed a pad from one long strip. Placing it on the wound, she bandaged Wade's shoulder, keeping it in place with longer torn strips. Pausing, she then removed the rest of his clothing.

His body was certainly different from Grant's, hard and toned. Wade was longer, his shoulders wider and his chest hairier, very masculine looking. A sudden jolt of lust gripped her lower body and she gulped air. It had been a long time since she had shared intimacy with a man, and the last few times with Grant had been dismal.

Making a pad of several blankets, she rolled Wade to one side and pushed them under him. Then she rolled him over the mounded edge and straightened the mattress of blankets to make them more comfortable.

She wrapped him in a clean sheet and piled blankets over him. "Keep the patient warm. Warm. Heating pad." She ran back upstairs. Plugging the heating pad in, she placed it between the blankets covering his chest. Wade groaned and she held her breath, but he subsided back into silence.

"I wish you would wake up." She watched his sleeping face.

How time and wisdom cleared a person's vision. Right now, he didn't convey the physically powerful and intimidating aura he had in his office. She was sure he used those undoubted assets to get whatever he wanted and grudgingly admitted to herself that he looked stunning. From the growth of his business, he must possess talent as an architect.

She thought of Preston's company letter in her purse. He seemed to be a businessman who apparently lacked scruples. She rose, retrieved the letter, and re-read it, frowning. *Wade deserved a superficial man-manipulator like Melissa.*

Amanda felt a stab of guilt. She knew no reason to malign Melissa Rillema, knowing little more than that she was endowed with all life's gifts—blonde, beautiful, blue-eyed, brains, and the money to make the most of them. Amanda knew from the announcement a year ago in the *Grand Rapids Press* that Melissa's father owned a huge development company out of Grand Rapids, making the forthcoming marriage more of a merger.

Fifteen minutes passed. She warmed milk on the electric stove, boiled water, and placed it on the stove to stay warm. Picking up the first aid book, she looked up frostbite, then bent over Wade and checked his face, hands, and fingers. He showed no signs but groaned when she wrapped her warm hands around his cold ones. His eyes squinted open, then opened wider.

"You!" The word erupted in a harsh whisper.

"I can explain…" She released his hands.

Wade's good arm rose, and his hand caught her around the back of her neck. He pulled her head uncomfortably close to his.

Giving up on explanation, Amanda offered reassurance.

"It's okay. You're safe."

He pulled her closer and kissed her, a soft, gentle touch, muttered something she didn't catch, then kissed her again.

This next kiss was not casual, or soft, or gentle. Her eyes closed and her lips seemed to respond of their own volition, rubbing and nibbling his. Eager purpose rushed through her body. Her hands cupped his face. Some movement made him groan…in pain. Her eyes flew open. *This is insane! He thinks I'm Melissa. Or perhaps thinks this is his last chance before he dies.* That thought brought her back to reality. She put a hand over her mouth as if to prevent a renewal of her assault, for her actions felt like a mugging. Her reaction embarrassed her. *Are you this desperate?* Wade's arm weakly dropped from around her as she pulled back. She tucked his arm under the blanket.

"I promise you: I did not shoot you!"

"Shoot?" He looked surprised, quickly followed by recollection flooding his face. "Call police." His voice was thick and slurred.

"Sorry, can't. Phone's out."

She jumped up from kneeling on the floor and poured cocoa into a cup. "You're lucky my mare, Noona, escaped from the barn and wandered into the back pasture. Otherwise, Buck never would have found you. You'd be lying in my orchard under the snow." She knelt and held a spoonful of cocoa to his lips. He neither opened his mouth nor looked like he believed her. His brown eyes were dark, overly luminous, and wary.

"I can account for every minute of my day since making that damn visit to your office! And you're suffering from hypothermia and need warm sweet liquids, so open your mouth."

He did, long enough to take one swallow. Grant had never done a thing she had requested without argument.

"Cell." His voice was weak and cracked.

"I don't have a cell phone, only a landline, can't afford one, and I told you, it's dead. Nothing unusual in this neck of the woods, especially in the middle of a bad storm." As if she commanded it, the wind blew in hard gusts driving pinging precipitation that rapped against the window. The lights went out with a clunking sound as the refrigerator's compressor stopped. Total quiet and pitch dark descended.

"No! Not now. Damn it! No!" Amanda rose, cocoa slopping over the cup's edge and onto her fingers. In seconds, her eyes adjusted. She saw the dim red-yellow glow from around the edge of the stove's burner door.

"Damn." Placing the cup on the floor to free her hands, she wiped them on her pants. She took several steps and felt her way along the edge of the sink counter. She skimmed her hands over the worn surface and found the flashlight. Switching it on, she pulled open a drawer, took out a candle and matches. Candle flickering, she used it to find the oil lamps in the utility closet and light them. Placing the lamps on the kitchen counter, she picked up the phone as she passed to check for a dial tone as she had every five minutes.

"Help me up," Wade ordered.

Startled, she looked at him. He struggled to rise.

"No way. Hypothermia can kill you. You lie there until you warm up. Besides, you might start bleeding again."

"Not hypothermia, just cold. Need to start your generator. You have one, don't you?"

"Or shock...you're probably suffering from shock. You stay horizontal for that, too. The generator is broken. It hasn't worked since last winter, well, maybe longer than that. Hopefully, the electricity will come back on soon."

Wade pulled the heating pad off his chest with his good arm and tossed it aside. Then, with a huge grimace, he pushed himself to a sitting position. Sheet and blankets fell to his waist, exposing his blood-smeared chest.

"You shouldn't do that." While she uttered the warning, Amanda appreciated his great-looking chest and abs. Her lips parted, she sucked in a slow breath.

Looking around the shadowed shabby kitchen, he said, "There's a cell phone in my jacket."

"Then why didn't you use it before you walked into my orchard to collapse?" Amanda walked to the plastic trash bag lying near the door and pulled out his jacket. She found no phone in any of the pockets.

"That's my jacket? Where are my clothes?" His outraged voice, as weak as it was, accused her of plans to keep him captive.

Amanda giggled then sobered. "Your jacket was too bloody to save, plus there is a huge hole in it. I took off your wet clothes. Don't take that off!"

Wade ignored her, took the scissors she'd left on the floor, and cut through the bandaging. He inspected the wound. It bled sluggishly. "It's not that bad. The worst went through the flesh, but I doubt if there is any bone involved. Nothing that won't heal. I'll live." He collapsed back on the blankets.

"Yeah. I can tell. It needs stitches. You just cut through one of my sheets. Now I need to cut up another. You're an expensive guest, Preston. You need a doctor, a hospital, and the police. I'll call as soon as the dial tone returns."

"No!"

Amanda remained quiet, considering his vehemence while she picked up the cup of cocoa. Everything remained shadowy in the lamplight, making it both uncomfortably intimate and hard to judge expression. She put one arm around his shoulders and helped him sit, held the cup for him to drink. He grabbed it from her and looked ready to toss the contents in her face but drank instead. His skin was smooth and warm where it rested against her arm, and she could see the muscles bulging along his good arm and shoulder. He handed her the cup.

"I didn't shoot you."

"I know you didn't."

"You thought I did out in the orchard. You know who did?" He didn't answer her. "Gunshot wounds have to be reported to the police."

He ignored her. She wondered if he was trying to dismiss her, or if reticence was his habit, but it irked her. The silence lengthened, accentuating the wind's howl outside the window.

"Is it still snowing?" he asked at last.

"Yes." She threw the bloody strips of sheet in the trash and started cutting another sheet.

"What are you doing?"

"Making bandages. First, I'm going to wash you, though."

"What time is it?"

"A little after midnight. Who shot you?" She poured some warm water into a basin and brought it to where he had reluctantly sunk back onto the pad of blankets.

"I don't know. My car skidded off the road...must have passed out. Left the car to find shelter...and help."

It took several minutes to clean the wound and the surrounding skin. She gently washed his face, arms, hands, and chest where blood had smeared his skin. He watched her, unnerving in his regard. When finished, she bandaged his shoulder and placed a blanket around his bare shoulders. "Your ankle is swollen. I had trouble getting your boot off. It might be sprained or broken."

"I remember falling a few times. The ground was treacherous."

"How far did you travel?"

"From my car, wherever that is." His brows scrunched. "Can't remember much except the road was slippery and visibility awful. Not sure, I may have seen some tail-lights passing me." He paused and then added, "If the electricity stays off for long, it's going to get cold."

"Not in here. The stove will keep us warm. I do have plenty of wood. Were you drinking?"

"What?"

"Before you got behind the wheel of your car. Had you been drinking?"

"No! I left from my office." He shivered. "You have anything to eat?"

She dished up some of dinner's stew, still warm from the thick-walled crock-pot, and held the plate while reminding herself to put the stew away. He rose to a sitting position and insisted on feeding himself. She placed the plate on the floor next to him and felt his forehead while he ate.

He pulled away from her touch, but when he finished eating, seemed exhausted. Amanda helped him lie down. Within minutes, he fell asleep. She touched his cheek, but he seemed normally warm.

She sighed and rose. It didn't look like the electricity was going to come on, which meant she had work to do. She brought in wood and stacked it in an old copper bin next to the woodstove. On another trip to the barn, she threw more hay into the stalls for the horses. Once finished, she searched for two dusty camp cots and cleaned them off. She lugged them to the house and set them up in the kitchen near the stove.

In another hunt, she found the sleeping bags and took the feather bed from one of the upstairs beds. She dragged everything to the kitchen. The feather bed fit over one of the cots and draped down the sides. As expected, the sheets would not fit well, but she made them work with safety pins.

Finished, she rose and saw a soft gleam in Wade's dark face. He watched her. "Good, you're awake. This will be better than the floor."

"I'm comfortable where I am."

She ignored him and walked over to stand looking down at him. "The floor will turn icy before morning. Think you can get up, or do I have to carry you over there, too?"

A flash of anger crossed his face. He swore, and sighed in defeat. "Damn bossy women."

She smiled. *Women.* At least she wasn't the only bossy one in his experience. With her help, he slowly levered himself up.

His hand clasped the sheet, bringing it up to cover himself as he rose. "I feel like someone used me for a punching bag."

"I had to drag you into the house," she said, putting a shoulder under his good arm. "Getting up the three steps from the back-door landing wasn't easy."

"Don't need help."

"That's what they all say before the fall."

He swayed on his feet. She picked up the excess sheet and wrapped it around him. With the tiniest smirk in her voice, she said, "You only have one good foot and one good arm. I don't want you falling and spreading more blood on my kitchen floor for me to clean up. I've a big enough mess as it is."

Not replying, Wade began his arduous journey to the makeshift bed. Barely touching his swollen foot to the floor, he hopped, tensing in pain with each movement. She guided him to the cot. "Drop the sheet," she ordered and helped him lie down, pulling his feet up onto the bed. He was exhausted, but it was warmer there. His feet were cold, and she started to worry. She layered him in blankets.

"You could have left me my shorts."

"They were stained with blood. They're soaking in soda water with the rest of your clothes. It might be nothing of a wound to you, but you bled a lot. Want something to drink?"

"Whiskey."

"Sorry. Milk, water, orange juice. Your pick."

"Cola?"

"Too much caffeine isn't good right now."

He sighed, settling back. "Water, then. Some aspirin."

"Okay."

He took the offering, swallowing the tablets and downing nearly the whole glass of water. He closed his eyes as if shutting her and the situation out. "I didn't expect anything like this."

"No one can foresee the unexpected."

After a few minutes, she turned and searched for the flashlight. She sighed with relief as a nice beam of light emerged from the end. Armed with the light, she went upstairs. Kari didn't wake as she carried her to the kitchen. The upstairs had already cooled significantly.

"The water. Damn."

She placed Kari in a sleeping bag on the other cot in the kitchen, fussing over her for a minute before zipping the bag. Her darling girl lay in the oblivious sleep of the young. Trying the phone, she swore and wanted to slam it down. Instead, she placed it softly in the cradle. Filling the stock and saucepots with water, she placed them on the limited counter space, thanking God that over the years enough pans had accumulated in the house. The water pressure dropped before she had finished filling all of them.

Grabbing the flashlight, she went to the basement. Buck, who had slept next to the stove the whole time, followed her. Only familiarity with the area and her anger kept it from becoming a scary trip. She slowed and placed each foot carefully on the shorter than normal stair steps.

She looked at Buck as he pushed by her and descended the stairs in a rush, tail wagging. "You're the only male I like. The rest are inconsiderate louts. He," she jutted her chin at her visitor upstairs, "would choose my property to try and die on—and look at the mess I'm dealing with." She turned off the pressure tank and opened a drain on the pipe.

"At least I remembered this before a pipe burst." She checked the water heater. "We have what water is left in the hot water tank." She patted Buck's head.

A check showed the furnace dead. The pilot light burned propane, but the electronic thermostat was off, so there would be no call for heat. Before going upstairs, she checked and locked all the tiny windows. Snow covered the glass in all of them.

"If I weren't paranoid before tonight, this evening would push me over the edge."

She went back upstairs. Buck followed. Wade snored softly. She felt his head, worried that perhaps he felt too warm.

She gathered all her houseplants in the kitchen. It would be warm enough at the furthest edges of the room to keep them from serious harm. To help keep the heat in the kitchen, she closed the kitchen door. She picked up the phone. *Dead.*

So was she, *dead tired.* She took one more run into the rapidly cooling upstairs, grabbed towels, washcloths, and the necessities for life, and took them to the kitchen. She spread the second sleeping bag over the braided rug in front of the sink and prepared for bed. As a last thought, she found two buckets, filled them with packed snow, and carried them to the bathroom off the kitchen. Settling in the sleeping bag at last, she sighed. The floor was hard, but Buck curled up behind her and she fell asleep. Her eyes opened at every sound, and even stone houses creaked in nighttime silence.

~ * ~

"Mommy, there's someone here."

"Ummm?" Amanda wasn't ready to wake up. It was too early.

"Mommy, it snowed out. It's cold."

Memory returned with a vengeance. Amanda rose to a sitting position in a single move, shushing Kari.

Darkness filled the window outside, and the wood stove held cooling embers. Frigid air filled the room.

She whispered, "Yes, honey, it snowed. It snowed so much the electricity went out. Mr. Preston was lost outside. Buck found him and we brought him home. You get back in your sleeping bag, sweetie. You'll stay warm there." She rose and carried Kari across the cold floor, placing her back into the sleeping bag. The chill seeped from the floor through her stockings.

Wade slept, but not peacefully. His skin felt dry and hot. "Damn, don't you do anything stupid like get an infection, Preston," she whispered. She flicked several wall switches on and off, but nothing happened.

She sighed. Picking up the receiver, she added, "And no phone." It took a few minutes to refill the cookstove with wood and get the fire roaring. Buck whined and she let him out and quickly closed the door to stop the draft of freezing air. Looking out the window, she noted the gray sky promised more snow. Snow already lay in a flat white carpet over the landscape, lining the trees and laying deep on the barn's roof. She judged the depth probably over her knees. She groaned. Her road, the back roads, would never get plowed today.

Three

"You have a radio?" Wade spoke in a low, weak voice.

His words broke Amanda's reverie over the view. She dropped the small curtain back into place and took the few short steps to the refrigerator.

"Electric only. The batteries went dead and I forgot to replace them." As she spoke, she took orange juice out of the fridge and poured it into three glasses. She gave one to Kari and carried the other to Wade.

"You ever hear of emergency preparedness?" He rose to lean on an elbow with one eyebrow cocked in irony, but he took the offered glass. Downing the juice in two large gulps, he handed her the glass, careful not to touch her.

Somehow, his untidy hair, sticking out at odd angles, and his unshaven, pallid face only added to his attraction. She liked him better this way—more manly than merely handsome.

"You want some more juice?"

"Please."

Amanda asked the nagging thought consuming her since the night before. "Will anyone come looking for you?"

He looked up at her, his face wearing a stricken look. After a few silent seconds, he said, "Maybe, but I don't think so. Not unless the road crew finds my car. Are you expecting any visitors?"

"No. Won't your fiancée or brother worry about you missing all night?"

"Don't have a fiancée, and I told my brother I was going to my cabin for a few days. No one will miss me. You own a snowmobile?" His gaze shifted to Kari.

His eyes shifted, and a chill ran up her midriff. He had been with Melissa only yesterday, and she hadn't looked like a cast-off woman. Had he broken off the engagement then? Or had she?

"Only one that doesn't work. What happened to Melissa? Last I heard, you were engaged."

He snorted. "A relationship like your generator and snowmobile—broken. How about a gun?"

"Sold." At his look, she said, "All of them. As you might very well know, I've had a few financial problems this past year."

"Since that scumbag you married ran off?" he asked.

Stiffening, she looked at Kari, but her daughter was not there. How had he known? The papers? He didn't know her at all, except for her land. Had he investigated her past? It didn't matter. She answered truthfully. "Yes. I used the proceeds to help pay my divorce settlement. I was also afraid of the temptation to use them. Consider yourself lucky."

Wade chuckled. Amanda gave him a nasty look. "I'll thank you not to talk about him like that in front of Kari. It's five a.m. You should go back to sleep."

"Why? Does she believe he's her father?" Wade's brows rose with his question, but his voice was a soft burr.

"No, and she knows who her mother was. I would not dishonor Marla's memory by denying her. The rest is none of your business. I don't want Kari to hear hateful talk for as long as possible."

She left to find Kari. "And your first try wasn't any better or worse than mine," she added in an undertone, sure he couldn't hear as she walked away.

Kari wasn't in the living room. "Kari? Kari? Are you upstairs?" she called up the staircase.

She heard Kari coming down the hallway to the steps before answering, "Mommy, the lights don't work. It's cold." She also carried a book and wore ballet tights and a tutu, her favorite outfit.

"This is a good idea," she said, taking the book and looking at the familiar cover. "We are both staying home today, and we'll need to entertain ourselves. The electricity is off. We need to stay in the kitchen to keep warm. Want some cocoa?" She shooed Kari ahead of her.

Once in the kitchen, she said, "Kari, this is Mr. Preston. He got hurt last night when he was out in the snowstorm. We must take care of him until we can get help. Right now, you stay in your sleeping bag until the stove heats up the room, okay?"

"But I want to play."

"Give me a few minutes to make cocoa, and I'll get you some warm play clothes. While these make you feel like a ballerina, they won't keep you warm enough." Once she had the teakettle on the wood-burning stove, she ran upstairs. Shivering, she gathered warm clothes from her room, then Kari's. In the spare bedroom, she looked in the old chest.

Some of her father's clothes remained in the drawers. She pulled out a flannel shirt, an ancient sweater, and an old pair of long underwear. At the bottom, she found sweatpants he had received as a gift but never worn. Finished, she rushed downstairs. She flung the men's clothes on Wade's cot and took Kari into the bathroom to put on the warm clothes, topping them with her bathrobe.

"This will help keep you warm. Put your socks and slippers on." Through the door, she heard Wade swear, and his hiss of pain, but she didn't return to the kitchen until Kari was finished.

Wade had managed to get the bottoms of the long underwear on by the time she returned but was struggling with the top. She pushed his hand away. He stilled. His gaze followed her every move. She did her best to ignore the sensation his attention brought. His expression turned unreadable. She dropped her gaze first, escaping the intensity of his. Her hands shook as she finished her task.

A quick check of the wound showed fresh blood. His ankle was bruised and swollen, and stretched the cuff of the long underwear bottoms. She cut the leg's hem open with a pair of scissors. Finished, she tore off another strip of sheet. It was quick work to make a sling for his arm. Then she gently worked the underwear top onto his good arm and over his head, pulling it down his chest. She heard his breath catch in pain as she stretched the fabric over his bad arm.

"I should have iced your ankle. I'm sorry."

He shrugged and groaned at his movement. "I was too cold then, and it's too late now."

"I'll get you some more aspirin. It might help. You have a fever." She held the shirt up, and he slid his good arm into the sleeve. She wrapped it around him and buttoned it.

Picking up the sweatpants, she cut the cuff before he slipped his feet into the legs. She helped him rise so he could pull them up.

"These Carter's?"

"No, they were my dad's. Everything of Grant's went to his parents or Goodwill."

"Thank you."

In his weakened state, he leaned on her, his greater height seeming to crush her shoulder.

"Sorry, too," he added.

"No need. I'd do the same for anyone."

"That's not why I'm sorry. I'm apologizing for the crack about Carter, and you're right. Neither my first attempt at wedded bliss, nor my recent engagement, worked out."

Amanda looked up at him, abashed. "You have very good hearing."

"Yeah. Sometimes, too good." His face expressed a hidden pain.

"Overhear something you shouldn't have?"

"In a manner of speaking, but it has nothing to do with my...our, present situation." He took one staggering step toward the bathroom, trying to not put weight on his swollen foot.

She tightened her grip around his chest. "Don't pull away. I won't let you get my property by suing me for personal injury."

He gave a weak laugh. "Wouldn't dream of it." He leaned on her as he moved. "Just so you know, I do appreciate everything you're doing for me, especially finding me."

"You're welcome."

When they reached the door, he said, "I can do this by myself."

"Give a shout if you can't. Don't flush."

"I know." He looked at the partially filled pails of water.

"Snow?"

"Yes."

He picked up one bucket, nodded, and closed the door.

Grandpa's cane was somewhere about. Where? Her mind wandered on to other matters as she tended the stove.

As she began to worry about how long he'd been in the bathroom, Wade opened the door. She helped him back to the bed. He had washed his face with the cold water in the pail. Wet spots liberally spotted the flannel shirt.

Contrite, she said, "Sorry. I should have told you I have heated water on the stove."

"I've washed in cold water before. You offered aspirin and cocoa?"

"Aspirin; didn't think you liked cocoa, but there is plenty. I think it's safe for you to have coffee or tea now if you prefer."

"I acquired a taste for cocoa last night," he said and smiled. "You know cocoa has caffeine?"

The truth dawned on her. "Oh, cripes. Well, you survived, so I must not have caused too much damage."

He smiled a devastatingly wicked grin. "I don't know about that."

She distracted herself, looking to see what Kari was doing. "Kari, do you have to go to the bathroom?"

"No. I already went."

"Did you flush?"

"Yes."

She must have made a face.

"Bound to have happened," Wade said. "No big deal."

Amanda nodded. "Kari, we don't have water to operate the pump until the electricity comes on, so we have to be real careful about water."

Kari nodded. "But that was toilet water."

"The water in the tank was clean. We could have used it in other ways." At Kari's expression, she added, "But that's all right."

"She couldn't have known, and we can bring in snow and let it melt."

Sighing, Amanda admitted, "True."

Amanda took the teakettle and went to the bathroom. Looking in the mirror was torment. Her hair was a ratty mess, and yesterday's mascara smudged the skin under her eyes.

Everything else remained familiar. Running the brush over her head, she pulled her hair into a ponytail before she washed her face. Finished in the bathroom, she used the last of the contents of one pail to flush the toilet.

Taking the pails, she detoured outside to fill them. Once back in the kitchen, she put her hands over the stove to warm them.

"I have to go take care of the animals. Kari, I have a chore for you. Up in the back bedroom closet is Grandpa's cane. Would you fetch it for Mr. Preston to use? And get some big, warm socks for him, too, from the bottom drawer in Grandpa's dresser," she added looking at his bare feet. "Take the flashlight with you. If you want some more toys, bring them down, too. Wear your coat, and do not stay up there, hear? And don't bother Mr. Preston." She picked her parka off the hook by the back door.

"Wade." He smiled at Kari and turned to her. "She won't bother me. Go do what you have to. Wear your coat, boots, and gloves, and don't stay out too long, hear?"

She made a face at his mimic of her mommy voice. Outside it was dark, cold, and crisp. No stars showed overhead, so it must be overcast, suggesting the snow wasn't finished. Grabbing the snow shovel, she scraped snow off the porch and down the steps. Buck stood on the porch watching her. As she finished the steps, she shouted, "Come on."

Buck barked a couple times, then bounded down the steps and through the snow. She watched him frolic as she shoveled. One leap took him into a drift where only his nose and the tips of his ears showed above the snow. Amanda laughed. Freeing himself in leaps and twists, Buck took shelter in the path cleaned behind her, shaking snow off his coat.

Settled, he followed her as she pressed through the snow to the barn. It was a struggle to get through the snow. In some places, it had drifted deeper than her thighs.

Once she made a footpath, she retrieved a bucket of water and a lantern from the house. She hoped the batteries hadn't died and damned herself for not purchasing extras. *Wade was right. I am unprepared for any emergency.*

The horses whinnied as she entered the barn, and she greeted each one, rubbing their long faces while she checked to make sure their blankets were properly strapped. After picking the stalls clean, she threw in some fresh bedding and placed extra grain and hay rations for them. She broke the ice covering Noona's and Ferd's water buckets before pouring in the water she had brought from the house.

Tina would be worried about her gelding. She rubbed Ferd, not feeling much through her glove, but enjoying the horse scent. "She'll be here, boy, as soon as the weather allows," she assured the animal. Ferd snorted but arched his neck to allow her glove to reach a certain spot.

Finished in the barn, Amanda decided to shovel a wider path back to the house. Daylight was brightening the horizon as she finished. Gathering an armful of logs from the woodpile, she stomped and scraped her boots before entering the house. Inside, she heard Kari talking in slow precise words. Smiling, Amanda realized she was reading.

"How much snow did we get?" Wade asked as soon as the door closed behind her.

"Looks like about twelve inches, maybe more, but it's drifting, and not done yet," she said. Ceasing her exertions made her dizzy. She caught her breath as she dumped the wood in the bin next to the stove. She exhaled and drew in a long breath before she returned to the entry to brush the snow off her jeans, hang up her jacket, and pull off her boots.

"I was about to send the cavalry out after you." Wade sat on a Windsor chair with Kari perched on his lap. His injured foot lay propped on a pillow on the chair next to him. He looked ragged, feverish, pale, in need of a shave, and his normally neat-as-pie hair was askew. Despite his illness, his dishevelment gave him a roguish charm.

"If you know how to contact them, please do."

Kari held a book. "I'm reading to Wade."

"I heard, and doing a very good job." Her glance caught Wade's; he enjoyed her daughter's company. It showed. Maybe he liked children. "I shoveled a path for your cavalry to get here."

"I watched. And wished I could help." Frustration filled his voice.

"Don't worry. Next storm, you'll be hale and hearty. I'll give you a call to come do my shoveling."

He laughed, his eyes crinkling with mirth. "That's a deal."

"Kari, set the table for breakfast, please." She glanced at Wade. "Are you up to bacon and eggs, Mr. Preston?"

"Yeah. Call me Wade, Amanda."

She resented the authoritarian tone, but the way he spoke her name..."Please?" he asked, like he'd read her mind. The humor in his face reinforced her thought.

Amanda laughed and nodded. "Good thing you added that 'please'."

Wade smiled. He swung his bad leg to the floor, so she gave orders in return. "Keep that foot up while you wait...Wade."

His gaze caught hers with an amused look. "I've heard my name uttered in more flattering tones. Go get some dry jeans first. It's too cold in here for wet clothes."

She checked the thermometer. "It's a balmy sixty-five. I'll throw some more logs on the fire." She refused to do as he said, and her legs grew cold when the damp jeans didn't dry. This was stupid, and only to prove she wouldn't be told what to do. *How childish.*

She served Wade and Kari before running upstairs to find a dry pair of jeans.

As she returned to the kitchen, she found Kari chattering to Wade. He listened with apparent interest.

Hearing her return, he looked up. "Kari's telling me about her daycare friends, and how her Grandma Gayle has been in Florida."

Amanda took her plate from the top of the stove where it had stayed warm. "Ouch!" The plate was very hot. She quickly put it down with the accompanying clatter of china against a hard surface. Grabbing an oven mitt, she lifted the plate and put it on the table, using the mitt to prevent the heat from damaging the table. She pulled out a chair and sat down. Kari and Wade were nearly done. Wade encouraged Kari to take bites between her words. Hungry, Amanda ate.

"So, this Jimmy, he is a friend?"

"Yeah."

"But he bruised your face?"

"It was an accident. He swung a toy at me and told the teacher he didn't see me."

"Well, maybe Jimmy should be more careful when he plays, or maybe you shouldn't play too close to him, huh?"

"That's a good idea!" Kari said, sounding like her Grandma Gayle.

Kari kept up her running conversation with Wade, asking why it snowed so much, and if the flowers were going back to sleep, and when could she go back to preschool. Amanda and Wade took turns answering. Their eyes watched the snow outside the window falling so thick it obscured the view. A half-hour later, the snow had stopped, and the sun shone.

After breakfast, Amanda suggested Kari go out and play for a few minutes. "Take Buck with you, he enjoys the snow. You can toss some snowballs and see if he will chase them." She helped Kari into her outdoor clothes, bundling her up. "Okay, out you go."

"Aren't you afraid she'll use Buck as a target?" Wade asked from the kitchen.

"She will, but he's faster than her aim is good."

She watched through the back door window a minute. Before facing Wade, she refreshed her tea and returned to the table with a determined air. "I want to hear what happened to you. This was no accident. I need to know if we—Kari and I—are in danger with you staying here. Will the person who shot you come looking to see if he can finish the job?"

Wade's lips tightened in what Amanda read as obstinacy before relaxing. He shook his head in a negative motion. "The snow has to have covered my tracks. No one could know you found me."

"Unless they followed you. That doesn't answer my question."

"If they had followed me, they would probably have finished the job already." His right hand ran furrows through his hair. He closed his eyes. "I don't know who shot me or why." He gestured to his shoulder, nearly growling in frustration. "I'd had a bad day. The night before, Melissa had called. I had broken things off with her months ago, but she asked me to wait until she told her family and friends. I was surprised to hear from her, and soon learned she wanted to change the status quo. She had never told her parents, and her father was talking about merging our businesses.

"The situation put me in a hell of a bad mood. I argued with Rodney before leaving for work and argued with Ed in the front lobby of our office. After not hearing what she wanted the night before, Melissa showed at my office, wanting me to escort her to some event in Grand Rapids, as if we had never discussed the end of the engagement over the phone. Then, you arrived."

"Let's see, your fiancée…"

"Ex-fiancée."

"Your business partner, your brother, and one of your property acquisition targets. Anyone you've not argued with?"

He sighed. "Doesn't seem like it. I left and went to one of our building sites. Ed met me there a little later. We talked about the solution to a few problems." He hesitated. "When we finished, I told him I was taking a couple days off and going to my cabin. After talking with Ed, I called Rodney and told him the same thing. My apartment is above the business, so I went back and changed. I had gone a few miles when a truck passed me. Something hit my windshield. I thought it must have thrown a chunk of ice up off the road, but something else hit the windshield and it shattered. I hit the brakes and the car skidded off the road and down an embankment. When I climbed out, I knew the car couldn't be seen from the road. Felt terrible, as though I'd wrenched my shoulder and started walking, felt liquid running down my arm. Pulled off my glove, saw blood, and knew I'd been shot." He looked at her and grinned. "Must have lost my bearings."

"Nothing funny about this."

His smile didn't falter...matter of fact, if anything, he looked happier. She did not believe him, or rather, felt there was a lot of the story missing. "Is there anyone you've made angry enough to shoot you?"

"You mean is there someone who wants to kill me? I didn't think so, but after this, who knows?" He fixed her with a steady gaze. "In mentioning the people who've been annoyed by me, you neglected to mention one. How about you?"

"I drive a twelve-year-old car, not a truck, and how would I know where you were or when you were going to be there?"

"Cell phone?"

"I stopped my service. Besides, who in your office called to let me know? What did the truck look like?"

"I don't know. I wasn't paying much attention. Blurs of snow-obscured color and taillights. The road was bad, and it was snowing hard."

"Think! Try to picture it."

He gave her an exasperated look. His gaze dropped to his mug of cocoa. "I have. All night...well what seems like all night. There is a lot of time I don't remember."

"You were unconscious a couple times."

They sat in silence a moment when Wade spoke. "I have a favor to ask you."

She looked at him in inquiry, but his regard remained on his cup.

"Don't let anyone know about this."

"About someone shooting you? Are you kidding?"

"No. Let me handle it."

"Gunshot—"

"—wounds are supposed to be reported," he interrupted, gazing at her intently. "But only by doctors and hospital personnel."

"You're ill with it. You might have an infection, and your foot surely needs medical attention as well. I'm sorry, but if anyone comes asking questions, I'll answer. Truthfully."

His gaze dropped. His gaze finally rose to her face. He smiled. "I know you will, fair enough. But if no one asks?"

"If no one asks, I have no reason to answer. But they will."

"By 'they,' you mean the police?"

"Yes."

He did not argue with her but fell into a thoughtful silence.

"You've no idea who might be behind this?" He grimaced but didn't answer.

"I need to know."

"No, you don't."

"You being here puts Kari in danger."

"No, I don't believe that."

"Either tell me the truth or as soon as the phone line is fixed, I'm calling the police."

"Don't be so damned inflexible!" His voice was low but held a definite growl.

She rose from the table, grabbing up his dishes. "I don't owe you any favors. You've damn near robbed me of all that I have left. I can't afford an attorney to fight you in court, and you know it!"

"Mommy?"

"Kari!" Amanda turned around. In a cheerful voice, she asked, "Did you have fun outside?"

"I'm cold. Are you angry?"

"No. Mr. Preston and I were discussing a problem we disagree about. Nothing to do with you, so don't worry. How about something hot to drink?"

Once she had Kari settled at the table, she asked Wade, "Do you want me to help you back to bed?"

"No. You have any reading material?"

She left and returned a few minutes later. While she was gone, he had moved back to the upholstered chair under the window. She gave him several novels Lark had given her and spread an afghan over his legs where they rested on the hassock in front of the chair. He sighed at the titles she handed him, but read the back cover blurbs before choosing one. He started reading.

Amanda sat next to Kari at the table. They colored pages from Kari's coloring book followed by a game of fish. She knew Wade watched and listened. The long morning dragged on. Eventually, Wade joined them in the card game and taught Kari a new one while Amanda made lunch.

By late afternoon, she noticed Wade looked ill and she made him lie down. He didn't resist and was asleep in minutes. She played with Kari until she put her to bed on the other cot.

Faced with a long evening, Amanda found her great-grandmother's journal in the bookcase in the living room. She sat in the upholstered chair Wade had occupied, thinking it somehow felt more comforting, as if the warmth of his body remained, before starting to re-read the journal. She kept a worried eye on Wade. He looked haggard and slept deathly still.

He roused a few hours later at the noise she made putting more logs on the fires. Catching his gaze, she asked, "I'm going to make some tea, can I get you anything?"

"Cola?" His lips looked dry.

She stuffed her grandmother's journal in a kitchen drawer to keep it out of the way, pulled a can from the pantry, and filled a glass while her tea water heated. He sipped the drink, his eyes glazed and heavy looking.

When her tea was ready, she curled up in the chair. The silence grew as Wade sipped his soft drink. After a few minutes, Amanda asked, "Do you like your work?"

"You mean displacing impoverished widows and their children from their family homes?"

She laughed. "I may be on the verge of being impoverished, but I'm not a widow. I meant being an architect and builder."

"It's been hard, and my company is only starting to reap the rewards of a good reputation, but yes, I do. How about you? Do you like working for Olson Bookkeeping?"

"I'm content, I guess. I had planned on becoming a horse trainer and continue showing our Morgans, but decided to get an associate degree in business and accounting to help Dad in the horse breeding business. Circumstances changed. I have a good income, even if I'm a little behind right now."

"I'm sure you'll turn around. I saw you ride."

"You did?"

"Yes. Back when you were in high school at a horse show in Traverse City. You were very good. As I remember, you took the blue ribbon."

Amanda sighed. "That was a long time ago. I hardly have time to ride now." She laughed. "And my only horse is too pregnant to ride."

"Do you think you'll go back to it?"

"Riding or my dream of training horses?"

"Both."

"Someday, yes."

"Why isn't your mother living with you? She didn't inherit?"

"My mom is my step-mom, but like I will be to Kari, she is the only mom I've known. When my dad died, we lived here together, but she met a great guy. Vic is a perfect companion for her, and I've come to love him, too."

"She had better luck than you had with Grant?"

"Way better." She regarded him a moment. "It was hard to face, but I eventually realized he only wanted me because I owned this property. He saw it as an easy street, not realizing the work involved in raising and training horses or operating an orchard. Not that he ever did any of that." Inhaling and letting her breath out in a sharp puff, she admitted, "I'm well rid of him, but it was an expensive lesson. What about your first marriage?"

He shrugged his good shoulder. "I found out she wasn't faithful. That ended the marriage for me. Luckily, there were no children, but like yours, it was an expensive lesson."

They talked quietly for another hour. The most enjoyable hour Amanda had experienced in recent years.

Later, lying on her pallet on the floor, disquiet kept her awake. Was she in danger of letting another man manipulate her with a show of false friendship? She may have had a teenage crush on Wade, but that didn't mean she had to succumb to his charm now. He had ulterior motives. His charm was not to be trusted.

Four

A piercing chill woke Amanda. Her nose and cheeks felt frozen and she shivered, though she was warm inside her sleeping bag. A quick glance showed the fire was out, although she could see and smell hot ashes in the firebox. The kitchen was frigid and very dark. She stifled her groan as she rolled and pushed herself to her stocking feet. The hard floor hadn't made a good mattress and felt like ice. Awaking in yesterday's jeans and sweatshirt didn't help, either. She felt grimy and disheveled. As she rose, she grabbed a sweater thrown on a chair and quickly shrugged into it.

Wade and Kari slept. She studied Wade's face. His pallor and the bruised look around his eyes spoke of his illness, but in the innocence of sleep, the strong lines and planes that composed his face belied any hint of treachery. *Don't fall for a beautiful face. Grant was handsome, and where did that get you?* Another side of her insisted Wade was different.

Moving quietly, she rebuilt the fire in the stove. The cold seeped through her stockings, freezing her feet, and her jaw trembled from shivering. Once the logs began burning, she raced to the rug in front of the kitchen sink, rubbing first one foot with the bottom of the other, then switching. She hugged herself.

Buck whined at her feet, wagging his tail. "Shush," she ordered and led him to the back door to let him out.

The animals needed feeding and the stove would need more wood soon. Since she was awake, she might as well start. She pulled on her boots, gloves, and coat before picking up a pail of melted snow water to lug to the barn.

It had snowed at least another six inches overnight. It was dark, but the sky had cleared, letting innumerable stars pinprick the sky with the Milky Way trailing across it in a wide arc. She picked out a few constellations her father had taught her as she waded through the snow toward the barn. Tree shadows lined the sparkling snow in the bright moon's reflected light. It was always colder when the sky was this clear, but seeing the stars and night shadows filled her with a sense of wonder. She sniffed the cold air, smelling the wood smoke from her chimney mixed with a frosty edge.

Not for the first time, she wondered how early settlers managed to endure the winters without furnaces, electricity, and piped water. Only a day or two without her normal conveniences challenged her enough. One of her greatest treasures was her great-grandma's diary, but although snowstorms were mentioned, how that lady had dealt with them wasn't written down. They were a part of daily life not worth noting in her journal. "Oh, Lord, I wouldn't have lasted. I'm glad for my many conveniences, don't think I'm not."

Buck thought she was talking to him and barked in agreement.

Inside the barn didn't seem any warmer than outdoors, but she knew the horses' shaggy coats helped keep them warm. She straightened Noona's blanket and felt the mare's rounded stomach. Amanda smiled when the foal moved under her hand. "How are you doing?" she asked. If it were a good enough foal, its sale would alleviate some pressing problems.

"Who am I fooling?" she asked the mare, stroking her muzzle. "By the time the foal is old enough to sell, it might be too late. My only chance is selling you." The thought brought tears and left her with a choking feeling.

Noona exhaled a frosty breath, whinnied, and turned to her hay net. The mare seemed fine. Amanda knocked the ice out of Noona's pail and refilled it with fresh water.

As Amanda left the barn, she heard the drone of a small engine. Instead of relief, the sound brought panic. The sky hadn't brightened with approaching dawn yet, although the black horizon had changed to navy blue.

Who could be out so early? Anyone she didn't expect was unwelcome. She hurried into the house, closed, and locked the door. Curiosity drove her to lift the back door curtain and watch. She shivered. The landing was warmer than outside, but cooler than the kitchen. Fear irritated her stomach and hastened her breathing. She continued to watch, remaining in her coat.

A snowmobile's headlamp pulled up near the porch step. The machine stopped by the back door. She let out a whoosh of relieved breath when the driver removed his helmet and the moonlight let her recognize him. Frank! She unlocked the back door and went into the kitchen with a smile on her face to start coffee in the old-fashioned drip pot she'd dug out of a closet the night before. She filled the base pot with water and set it on the cookstove to boil.

Within minutes, Deputy Frank Teigman, her best friend's husband, came in after a brief knock. She watched him from the kitchen door as he put his helmet on the bench under the coat rack. "Hi, Amanda." He smiled as he unzipped his parka.

"Hello, Frank," Amanda said. "You're out early. I'm making coffee." She looked at the pot, seeing the water had risen into the coffee chamber, and pulled the pot off the stove.

"Lark asked me to check on you. Thought I'd come by before going to work. Sorry if I woke you." He pulled off his gloves as he stamped and wiped his boots on the door-side rug.

"You didn't. I've already been out to the barn."

He grinned, and she backed from the entry to let him into the kitchen. "Good to see you survived." He walked to the stove and held his hands to the heat with a sigh. "Ahh, that feels good."

His voice changed as he observed Wade Preston staring at him from where he had risen enough from the cot to lean on his good elbow. Frank's gaze shifted to Kari asleep on the other cot. He lowered his voice so as not to wake Kari. "I came to see if you needed help, but I didn't expect anything like this. Looks like another of Lark's hunches hit pay dirt. Preston? What's he doing here?"

Before Amanda could answer, Wade sat up, slowly swinging his injured foot to the floor.

Amanda looked at Wade and bit her lower lip before speaking one notch above a whisper. "Wade Preston, Frank Teigman. Deputy Frank Teigman." She made the brief introduction and turned away as she removed coffee cups from an overhead cabinet, asking, "How bad it is out there, Frank? Any idea how long the electricity will be out?"

The smell of brewed coffee filled the kitchen. She poured the coffee into three cups.

Frank leaned against the sink counter as Wade slowly rose. Frank's steady gaze took in the arm encased in the shirt and the cane Wade used to help himself stand. "Electricity may come on sometime today. Ice took down quite a few power lines. Lots of trees down, too. No promises from the utility company. The phone might be longer. Power crews are working on it. Some parts around here got fifteen and more inches of snow. Drifting is bad. All schools are closed, and all activities have been called off." He took a breath and looked at Amanda. "Lark figured you were stuck out here. Been yabber'n at me since yesterday morning to come over."

Frank looked at Wade. "You've been reported missing. Search parties are being assembled to look for you. Some snowmobilers spotted your car late last night."

"Car slid off the road."

"It's about a mile down Red Apple Road. Everything okay here, Amanda?" Frank asked.

"Wade injured his ankle, lost his mobile phone. He's been stranded here by the snow."

"Lucky he made it to your house. Found blood on the driver's seat of his car and a .38 casing in the padding. Upset a few people," Frank said, as deadpan as if it were a common occurrence.

He abruptly walked to the back door landing, pulling his police radio out of a pocket in his parka. He shut the door behind him, but they could hear him and the crackle of dispatch's response.

"Dispatch. This is Mobile One. I've found Preston. Cancel the impending search. Yeah. He's okay, stranded like a lot of others, so couldn't contact anyone. Lost his cell while walking to a house in the storm. Yeah. I'll talk to you when I get to the office."

Wade looked grim as Frank returned. Amanda refreshed the cooling mugs with hot coffee.

There was a brief lull as the men sipped their coffee.

Wade looked at her. "Can I talk privately with Deputy Teigman?"

"Where do you want me to go, Wade, the barn?" She threw up her hands to stop his reply. "Never mind. Buck needs to walk anyway." Before pulling on her boots and coat, she checked Kari, who remained soundly asleep. Snapping her fingers for Buck, she told the two men. "Keep your voices down and put more wood on the fire as needed."

She stomped out of the door. "Come on, Buck."

With nowhere else to go, she returned to the barn. Buck raced around her and leaped through the snow. Inside, Noona turned in her stall to face Amanda, her soft eyes inquisitive. Both horses chomped their hay, the sounds of their munching filling the air. Amanda watched them before taking Ferd from his stall.

Opening the rear barn door wasn't too difficult, but the snow was very deep. The indoor riding arena stood twenty feet from the barn. The snow was deep but walkable. The newer arena door slid open easier. She released the gelding into the arena where he could get some exercise. He walked a few steps then leaped and ran, jumping and bucking with Buck at his heels, barking. Their chase didn't worry her as it was a common game they played.

A minute later, she released Noona. The mare ambled around the enclosure. Another trip provided hay for the two horses. After a few minutes, Amanda, shivering, jumped up and down and waved her arms to stay warm.

"This is too damn cold," she said to the horses. "I'll come back in a couple hours." She left the arena and returned through the barn to the path to the house.

Frank stood outside by his snowmobile waiting for her to return. He put away his radio as she approached. "I've called Doc Meyers. He'll come out. I'll bring him here." His attention turned to adjusting his helmet and putting on his gloves. "You be careful," he told her. "Preston's not giving you any trouble, is he? According to Lark, you two aren't the coziest of friends."

"We're getting on just fine. Considering the situation, and if you think it's safer, he can stay here."

Frank's eyes creased in speculation. "Don't know, but I expect it is. It'll be at least tomorrow before the road gets plowed this far." He grinned. "Course, anyone with a snowmobile can get in. So, I repeat, you be careful."

"Yeah, you scared me, but thank you for coming to check on Kari and me."

"Sorry I scared you. I figured I might, coming this early, but Lark was worried."

As they stood there, the outdoor floodlight came on. Inside lights turned on, making the house seem warmer, more welcoming. Glimmering crystals of snow and ice reflected all around the windows.

"Well, looks like you're lucky. Now you can leave the kitchen," Frank said, straddling his machine. "I'll be back in about an hour or so with the doc, if possible. It'll be daylight by then, but I don't imagine we'll draw much notice." He started the engine.

"You have to report this?"

He gave her his calm regard. "When I know what *this* is, and what the good doc says, yes, I will."

Amanda nodded and waved him off, watching his machine slide easily over the deep snow. Buck would not come in. He looked at her, then bounded away, daring her to chase him, his dark shape seeming to float against the white ground. "Fine. Stay out," she snapped, closing the door.

Inside, Wade sat alone at the table staring at the wood surface. Kari remained asleep.

"Frank said he would be back soon," she said. Wade said nothing. "I'm going to the basement to check the furnace and turn on the pressure tank." Matching her actions to her words, she fled from her own kitchen, ignoring Wade's low-voiced, "Amanda!"

The furnace plenum already hummed with burning propane. She turned on the water tank and listened as the pump started drawing water. Opening the washtub faucet, she left it open until water gushed out. Gurgling sounds ran through the water pipes lining the ceiling before settling into a quiet flow of water. Upstairs, she heard Wade hopping to the kitchen sink, opening the faucet, and heard the water groan through the lines. She saw the bucket of bloody clothes near the washer and dumped them in the utility sink to drain. Wringing them out, she shoved them in the washer and started the load.

Thinking she had procrastinated long enough, she went upstairs. Wade sat at the table, pain lining his face. He looked feverish.

"I put your clothes in the washer. I think the blood soaked out and won't leave any stains."

He looked at her with the lines around his eyes deeper and more evident. "Sit down."

She jerked in response. No one bossed her around, not anymore. He caught the motion and a fleeting smile crossed his face.

"Please."

The 'please,' though slightly belated, plus pure curiosity, brought her feet to the table without argument. She sat and then jumped up. "Give me a few minutes. I want to put Kari in her own bed. I need to make something warm for Doctor Meyers and Frank. They'll be cold. You think coffee? Maybe cocoa would be better."

She lifted Kari, sleeping bag and all, and took her to her bedroom. Already the furnace was pouring hot air into the room. The room remained cold, but it would heat up fast, and Kari would be warm in her sleeping bag. She fussed for a moment to make sure Kari was all right. *Tired baby. I let her stay up so late.*

Wade remained at the table, but he raised his head from where it rested on the palm of his good arm when she entered. Only his gaze moved, following her movements. He waited to speak until she poured herself coffee and refreshed his cup and made a fresh pot, this time in the machine. As she took her first sip, Wade said, "You want to know you're safe, that Kari's safe. Like I said, and Frank Teigman agrees with me, no one could know you found me. Any trace of my coming here is buried under a foot of snow. Please believe me when I tell you how grateful I am that you did find me, and how sorry I am to put you in this situation."

"Who shot you?"

"I don't know. I'm afraid to speculate, but things have been going on in the company."

"What things?" she demanded.

"Things I was blind to until almost too late." He cleared his throat. "I discovered our financial sheets didn't add up. A little investigation showed a large sum of money was unaccountably missing from a reserve account."

"Is that why you're so eager to get my land? To shore up some financial disaster your company is suffering?"

"Your land plays a small part in the plan my company developed and in the economic growth of the whole area."

"I've seen the plan. Condominiums to the north of me. Are you planning to put some on my land, too?"

"Your farm is not profitable, but the back acres have a great view of Lake Michigan. That view is worth a chunk of money and is wasted on an unproductive apple orchard."

"My farm's profitability is my business! It was thriving until I had to pay a different leech sucking the profit from it! It will thrive again."

Anger flared in his eyes, the lines of his face firming, harshening. "Don't compare me to Grant Carter! Look at this house! Look how you're living. Your kitchen is a conglomerate of add-ons and worn-out cabinetry and counters. The sink, refrigerator, and stove are decades out of date. A solution to your financial woes is right in front of you, and you refuse to take advantage of it!"

She inhaled a deep breath, steadying her temper. "I don't need to look at this house. You look at it. My father was born upstairs, and so was his father! My great-grandma cooked at the cookstove that has been keeping us warm, and these stone walls have sheltered my family all that time. This is where I choose to bring up my daughter."

"But she's not your daughter, is she?"

Struck afresh, she stared at him. "Yes, she is. I legally adopted her."

"She's your cousin's child. It's what broke up your marriage, isn't it?"

"You must listen to every gossipmonger in town. Yes, Grant didn't want children, especially someone else's. But Gayle showed me how much a mother could mean, and I couldn't let Kari go into foster care or be adopted out of the family. There wasn't anyone else. Marla's parents both have health problems, and although they would have taken Kari, it would have placed an enormous burden on them. What broke up your marriage?"

Wade held her gaze, but the lines in his face firmed and he swallowed hard. "I'm not sure what broke us up. I suppose we both stopped trying. I came home early one day and found another guy with her. That was it. All I was trying to say is Grant was always a selfish bastard and a poor sport. When will you finish punishing everyone else for it?"

Don't let him goad you!

Scratching at the door gave Amanda an excuse to rise and let her temper cool. She went and let Buck in. The air that entered was remarkably warmer than it had been. Looking out, she saw melting already taking place. Icicles dripped water all along the porch eves. Buck shook the snow off his coat, spattering her before he trotted off to the rug in front of the sink. She walked back to the table, glancing around the kitchen.

She sat and looked at Wade. "I don't blame you for Grant's choices. You are what you are."

"What, a man?" He sighed and rubbed his forehead as if he had a headache. "This isn't getting us anywhere. I'm trying to explain things to you, so let's try not to get sidetracked."

Amanda swallowed her first comeback and stared at Wade a moment. Was that how she came across, as a bitter, vindictive man-hater? She sighed. "You're right. Who do you suspect? Your best friend or your brother?"

His expression changed so quickly that Amanda felt a pang of sympathy. He looked about to cry. That shook her. She softened her tone. "I suppose one choice is as bad as the other. Maybe it's not either of them."

He snorted, looking into his cup, and took a sip while visibly composing himself. He turned a tormented gaze to her. "Rodney is always asking for money, for a raise, for a loan. But Edward is the company's accountant. I don't want to believe or accuse either of them of attempting to kill me. I don't want to start an official investigation that could lead to their arrest."

"You have to. Frank said the police know someone, at least, shot at you. He won't turn a blind eye to a gunshot injury, not for long." She put a hand over his. "Let the police handle it. If you have to face either choice, you can give them your support and forgiveness."

He looked away. "I don't think I can face them. Not when every time I see them, I'll remember the suspicions I have."

"You don't have to face them, not right away, anyhow."

Noise from a snowmobile broke the silence. Amanda looked at the clock, judging the time seemed to have passed too quickly. She looked out the window. Grey light was starting the day, but the clouds covering the sky didn't threaten more snow.

"They made faster time than Frank thought."

"Or it's not Frank," Wade replied.

Amanda stood at the back door with the curtain pulled aside far enough to ascertain who was coming. With a sigh of relief, she unlocked and opened the door. Doctor Meyers pulled off his snowmobile helmet and entered with a warm smile. After greeting her, he pulled off his gloves and hat.

Amanda closed the door as Frank remained near his machine, speaking on his radio. "You were quick. Thank you for coming."

Doc Meyers kicked his snow-covered boots off near the door, unzipped his jacket, and pulled the straps of the bibbed, insulated pants off his shoulders. "My office was closed yesterday, and Frank caught me on the way home from West Shore Medical. Someone always goes into labor during a storm."

Frank came in as the doctor took the steps to the kitchen. He gave her a nod as he took off his jacket and unzipped his bibs, but he wasn't smiling. She went into the kitchen.

"There's coffee, or I can make cocoa, whichever you prefer."

"Coffee's fine," the doctor said, and Frank nodded.

She put clean mugs on the counter and placed the sugar bowl and the carton of milk from the refrigerator next to the cups and spoons. "Help yourself. I've got to go upstairs and check on Kari."

Amanda left, giving the men privacy. Kari slept, overtired from the changes in her schedule the last few days. In her own room, Amanda made her bed with fresh bedding and put extra towels in the bathroom, all the time wondering what the men in her kitchen were saying. Doubting Wade would leave, she pulled clean sheets and blankets from the linen closet. Normally, she would have given a guest her father's bedroom, but Wade couldn't manage the steps. He could sleep on the couch, which would be marginally better than the cot. She trusted Frank to protect her interests, but that didn't diminish her curiosity. Sighing, she grabbed the pile of linen for the living room couch and went downstairs.

Wade, bare-chested, the flannel shirt unbuttoned and half off one shoulder, sat in one of the kitchen chairs. Doc Meyers held the shirt while Frank took photographs of the wound. Wade must work out. No one had muscles like that without effort. Certainly not Grant. She felt fifteen, seeing Wade on the football field from the sidelines, feeling the passion of her hero worship, knowing he was never going to look at her.

But he has looked at you. She inhaled a short breath. That thought made a mess of her rational world.

After Frank finished recording the wound, Doc Meyers gave Wade an injection, over vehement claims from Wade that he was fine.

"Yeah. Heard it before. Amanda, you have an extra bed for him? Wouldn't leave him here but can't get him out on a snowmobile and an ambulance can't get in here."

"Could have a Med-Evac helicopter come," Frank said.

"No." Wade's words overrode Frank's before the officer finished speaking. He looked at the doctor. "You said I'm in no danger, wound appears clean, and you've given me antibiotics. Amanda has agreed to let me stay here. Haven't you, Amanda?"

The blatant assumption ignited her anger, but looking at the expectation on Doc Meyers' and Frank's faces, and seeing Wade's imploring expression, she ignored her irritation. He wasn't ready to face his brother and best friend. That was understandable.

"He can use the sofa, or Dad's bedroom if he can get up the stairs. It should be warm by now."

"It would be a good thing to get that wound and ankle X-rayed." At Wade's expression, Doc Meyers looked at the staircase. "Down here is better."

"I can move the cot to the living room..." Frank offered.

Wade interrupted. "The sofa's fine, but I'd like to take a shower."

The doctor and Frank helped Wade stand and assisted him upstairs. She followed them and continued to her father's room where she found more clean clothes. Knocking on the bathroom door, she handed the clothing to Frank.

A few minutes later, she heard the shower come on, and Amanda hoped there was enough hot water to last. She pulled the sheets and blanket off his cot and turned the sofa into a bed. While she cleaned the kitchen, she heard the men come downstairs. Frank joined her shortly, his look questioning.

"It's all right, Frank. He can stay here until you find out who is responsible for injuring him."

"It might be safest for now, Amanda."

Doc Meyers walked into the kitchen. "He's on the sofa. I gave him something to make him sleep," he said. "He needs rest. Keep him in bed the rest of the day and keep that foot up." He pulled some sample packets from his bag. "Have him take one of these tablets every twelve hours. The other is for pain. No more than one every four hours."

Both men started pulling on their outdoor gear.

"I have to take Doc back to his car, Amanda, and check in with the office, but I'll be back later to get a statement from you." He dug into his parka's pocket and handed her some batteries with a sly grin. "Put these in your radio. You really need to update your technology and move into the twenty-first century. You'll be glad to hear the forecast says we may have temperatures in the sixties."

She smiled and nodded. "Can't promise to do better the next time, but I'll try to at least have batteries in the house."

Frank shook his head with disbelief. The two men left. Within minutes, she heard the snowmobile pull away from the house. While she made a cup of tea, she heard the television come on. She took her cup and went into the living room. Wade half lay, half slouched on the couch, drowsy looking, watching an early morning program. When the local news came on, the lead story was about the disappearance of a local businessman, Wade Preston. Short clips showed brief interviews introducing Melissa as his fiancée, Edward, his partner, and his brother, Rodney, expressing their grave concern.

Wade said nothing, but his face revealed his stricken guilt. He must have resolved whatever bothered him, for his expression became sober-calm, and before long, he fell asleep. Amanda pulled the blanket over his shoulders as she heard Kari upstairs. Thank God she had slept through all the commotion.

Five

A familiar rumble woke Amanda. Somewhere in the recess of her mind, the sound registered as the truck of Wyn Pootsma, Tina's dad. He always cleared her drive before his other plow jobs. Recognizing the sound, she snuggled in the warm comfort under her covers. *Plowing!*

Smelling coffee at the same instant as she recognized the noise outside, she opened her eyes. Sleep hadn't refreshed her, even after going to bed exhausted and sleeping like the dead, but she jolted awake. Rolling onto her back, she stretched, wanting to go back to sleep, but rose instead. A slice of light escaped the side of the window's shade and highlighted the side table. She checked her clock. *Five to eight. How could I have overslept?*

Leaping from bed, she grabbed her bathrobe and rushed down the hall while she pushed her arms through the sleeves. Kari's bed was empty and so was the bathroom. In the living room, the sheets and blankets lay neatly folded over the empty couch. She found Wade in the kitchen balancing on one foot, the cane lying against the counter, pouring milk into two bowls. Kari sat cross-legged on the table, giggling.

Caught unaware, Amanda swallowed the sudden thickness in her throat. This homey scene epitomized everything she wanted for Kari and for herself, and Wade was perfect in the role.

She stood, silent and unnoticed, surveying the scene, and saw in a flash that Wade was right. The kitchen looked shabby. The worn varnish on the old oak floor left dull patches amid the shiny. The teapot motif wallpaper looked faded, drab—and cheap. Old and worn handmade cabinets lined the room. A gold-colored electric stove from the seventies sat opposite the old wood-burning cookstove. At the other end, next to the upholstered chair occupying the window space, an ancient oak table served as both a work surface and dining table. Mismatched chairs graced the table's sides. Like the rest of the house, the kitchen worked but needed work.

With no fire in the stove, the room felt cool, the thermostat set low to preserve fuel. She tugged the belt on her robe, unsure if it was warmer or colder than when the furnace had been off. The sight of Wade making himself at home in her kitchen, fixing breakfast for her laughing daughter, made her both shiver and sweat. *This was taking a high school crush a bit too far!*

"Good morning," Amanda said, walking to the kitchen counter. She went to the window behind the table and looked out. Wyn's truck was pushing the snow into mounds.

"Morning, Mommy. Wade called me a cricket fairy."

"Morning, Amanda." Wade turned his head to look at her from where he leaned against the counter with lined up the bowls and glasses already lying on it. He took a mug from the cupboard and poured coffee.

"You look better. How do you feel?" she asked.

"Better. Medications and a good night's sleep seem to have helped." His red-rimmed eyes didn't look any more rested than hers felt. And she felt ragged rather than refreshed.

"You're fixing breakfast?" she asked Wade the obvious, turning to Kari. "What's a cricket fairy?"

"Just cereal," Wade answered, closing the box top. He turned from the counter and picked up the cane. "A cricket fairy is a princess-elf-girl who jumps around like she has wings and chirps a lot."

Kari giggled.

He held out the mug. "Here, coffee."

Amanda drank the hot brew walking to the window to watch the plowing. She turned and scooped up Kari and placed a kiss on her head. Putting her down on the floor, she told Wade, "I don't know how you can get a good night's sleep on that couch. Here, Kari, help carry these bowls to the table." She handed one to Kari and glanced at Wade.

"How are you feeling?" he asked.

"Rested." *Lie.* The coffee was perfect. "Did Kari wake you?"

His charming smile beamed toward Kari. "In a most enjoyable way—with feathers and giggles. Your plowman has been here about fifteen minutes. There's a girl in the barn."

With the cane, he limp-hopped to the table. The grimace he wore when he sat told Amanda he was not as well as he claimed.

Amanda pulled orange juice from the refrigerator. "Tina. She stables her quarter horse gelding, Ferd, here in exchange for taking care of the animals and delivering supplies. She barrel races with him. We split the cost of feed and bedding. It's a good solution to both of our problems. Especially since her dad plows my drive for free. I've leased my orchards to him. He owns more north of town."

"That's a huge barn."

Amanda smiled. "That's only half of it. There's a riding arena behind it. My father had the arena built back in the eighties. He put more money into restoring the original barn than good sense dictated, but he loved that old structure. Said it had a unique character. Tina will let Noona and Ferd into the arena to exercise."

"You inherited when your dad died?"

She hesitated, wondering at his interest. "He suffered a heart attack after an automobile accident. My brother died in the same accident. I think Dad blamed himself, although the crash wasn't his fault. Gayle received his life insurance, and he left me the farm."

"And Grant took advantage of your grieving state?"

She didn't answer and tried not to react while she poured orange juice. *Was it true? Had grief made her blind to Grant's motives?*

And how could Wade know the timing of events, unless he had her investigated? She delivered the juice to the table.

"I met Grant at my dad's funeral. He said he was there on behalf of his father, who had served in the Vietnam War with my dad. He offered to help and came here every day. We just slipped into marriage. Would you like some eggs and toast?"

He held a spoon full of Lucky Charms above his bowl. "Just toast, and more coffee—please."

After putting bread slices into the toaster, she refilled their coffee. Replacing the coffee carafe, she looked out the window. Sunlight sparkled on an unbroken blanket of white, and the snow-lined tree branches etched a black filigree against the silver sky. It looked beautiful—freezing, but gorgeous. "Frank said it was going to start warming up, but it hasn't yet, at least not much."

She felt Wade's gaze on her as she stood by the counter, and he chatted with Kari. When the toast popped up, she buttered it, came to the table, and sat down before she smiled. "They must have cleared the road during the night."

"Are you anxious to get out?" Wade asked.

She looked at him. "You aren't?"

"Not particularly."

"Because of the situation?"

His smile was like sunshine. "That and the pleasant company."

"Ha." Amanda returned him a one-sided smile of disbelief as she felt a blush heat her face.

"Are you going into work today?"

The phone rang. Without answering him, Amanda picked up the receiver.

"Amanda?"

She recognized the voice. "Hi, Nan. Drive's being plowed as we speak."

"Not to worry. Don't come in. I meant to call you last night. Something is wrong with the furnace at the office. It's freezing. I'm waiting for the repair service to call back. I'll call when it's warm enough to come in."

"That's too bad. You think the repairs will be finished today?"

"No. Brad said to wait until tomorrow morning to come in, but I'll call you."

"Well, he's the boss. Thanks for letting me know."

She finished talking with Nan and put the phone down. "I won't be going to work until tomorrow, but once I shovel my car free, I'll drive you to the medical center to get X-rays."

Wade studied his coffee cup, one hand curled around its curves. Kari had left the table. Amanda heard the television in the living room.

"Eager to get rid of unwelcome company?" he asked with one raised brow.

"Not at all." It surprised her, but she spoke the truth—a dangerous truth. Everything she thought and felt seemed mixed up and topsy-turvy. She hated that he had awakened her adolescent yearnings, made her want more than just companionship, that he made her think about forgiving him for the grief he had caused her...but having another adult in the house, even Wade, had been bliss. Caring for him had ignited a long dormant longing. That he had been nice to Kari was only sugar-coating her reaction. "If you want to hide out for a few days, you must know a better place than here." As she made her offer, she wondered what was wrong with her mind.

His smile was crooked. "I'll call Rodney after breakfast. He'll come pick me up." His face took on a harder expression. "Would you show me the letter you received from my office?"

She shrugged. "Sure." Finding her handbag, she pulled out the envelope and laid it on the table next to him.

Wade removed and unfolded the letter. As she watched him read, she blurted out her suspicion. "You didn't write it, did you?"

"No. I didn't." His face darkened and his expression became unreadable. "I would have come to talk face-to-face before ever threatening to go to the planning department and seek condemnation. I doubt if they would grant eminent domain anyhow. If I hadn't been so angry and distracted with both Edward and Melissa when you came storming into my office, I wouldn't have reacted the way I did." He gave her a rueful smile and added gently, "However, that doesn't change the fact that this county needs this project. It not only provides employment but will bring people into the community. That brings economic growth."

"And puts me out of my home."

"The proceeds from the farm's sale would provide for you and Kari—"

She cut him off. "Kari and I live a very simple life. One that suits the two of us."

His single raised brow expression returned. "One in which you don't need a man?" Before Amanda could come up with the scathing retort his question deserved, he quickly added, "That was rude. I'm sorry."

"It's not that hard doing without one."

He laughed. "What would you know about doing without?"

"Look around. According to you, I know all about it."

Wade winced. "I'm sorry for that crack, too. There is nothing wrong with this house. It shows wear, but it also has a homey charm missing in many newer houses."

"Is your home on the lake all sleek and modern?"

He huffed a single laugh. "I live in a loft apartment above my office building done in a modern industrial style selected by a professional decorator."

"Not homey?"

He shook his head. "Hardly. But it works for my business. So does the decorator."

"Perfect for a bachelor?"

He put on a charming, self-effacing grin. "Pretty much."

The phone rang as he seemed about to say more. Amanda reluctantly rose and answered. At first, she didn't recognize the voice. When she did, shock kept her silent for a moment, allowing her caller to burst into rapid speech. She snatched a quick breath and interrupted. "I don't want to hear anything you have to say, and I have nothing to say to you. Don't call me!" She hung up the phone with a curious gentleness for all the anger she felt.

It took a moment to manage her emotions before she turned to face Wade. She had not looked at him except at the very start of the phone call when she saw his interest and the stiffening of his body, likely in reaction to her own expression. Sitting at the table, she reluctantly regarded him.

Wise man, she thought looking at his face. His eyes displayed his curiosity, but his firmly pressed lips refused to blurt any questions. She couldn't read what the taut lines on his face meant.

She explained without his asking. "That was my ex. Grant must have heard about your offer for the land. I'm sure he thinks he deserves a share."

"He's pressing you to accept the offer?"

"I don't know. I didn't listen. He probably knows I'll lose it if I don't pay my taxes." She sighed. "I didn't know he was back in town."

"Your taxes are only delinquent. You have until next April to catch them up."

"Plus interest and penalty, plus the next year's taxes." Her eyes watered. She swiped one finger under her left eye to wipe away an incipient tear, not wanting to show any vulnerability in the face of the enemy. "Your partner must have waited until he could confirm I missed the February due date before he sent his letter."

Wade looked away, not meeting her questioning gaze. "He must have. Ed is good at pointing out the obvious and applying the logical solution...and pressure. From your tax statement, I assume you must have an idea of the value of your land. He offered a substantial amount over that."

"Does only monetary value count?"

He gave her a look measured by contemplation. "No, if you can afford to ignore it. This is Ed's project. I haven't been following all the details."

"Without lake frontage, my land isn't that valuable."

"He already has other lake frontages. I promise you, I'll look into this."

Her breath caught in her throat, stopping any speech. Kari came into the kitchen. "I want to go outside and play."

The sound of plowing had stopped. "Okay. Get your things on." Amanda helped her. "Take Buck with you." Buck heard and rose, shaking himself before trotting over, his tail wagging.

After helping Kari with her snowsuit and boots, she opened the back door and let them out. The sun glared off the snow. Tina waved from the barn as she walked to her dad's truck and shouted, "Stalls are cleaned, Ferd and Noona fed and watered."

Amanda waved back and shouted, "Thanks."

Tina jumped into the passenger side of her dad's truck and slammed the door shut. Her father drove away. It felt like a lifeline of normalcy dragging out of reach, so different from the tumult in her kitchen, in her mind, her heart, her very life. She suddenly wanted Wade gone, wanted her safety back.

Amanda heard dripping water. A glance showed drops falling from melting icicles along the eaves. Buck bounded around the cleared drive. She looked at Kari. "Stay in the yard, okay?"

She closed the door. Picking up one of the empty buckets from near the bathroom door, she placed it next to the wood-burning stove.

"I need to empty the ash out of the stove and fireplace." She was unsure from where the strong desire to accomplish the ugly task came.

"In your pajamas?"

"No." Heat suffused her face as she felt self-conscious and ridiculous. "I'm going right now to change. I'll pour you more coffee first." As she set the cup on the table, she caught his gaze. "I don't want to sell."

In her room, she quickly pulled on an old sweatshirt and a pair of jeans with ragged hems. Back in the kitchen, she found Wade had pulled a chair to the stove side and carefully emptied shovels of ash into the pail. He glanced at her while he carefully removed another shovel full of ash.

"Found the fireplace shovel, thought I could do something to earn my keep."

"No need. You were good company when I needed it."

"Taking care of a wounded, storm-lost straggler?"

"I don't like storms, even when home. You kept my mind from worrying about everything else that could have gone wrong."

Wade's cheeky grin reappeared. "You worry too much."

"I have a lot to worry about."

"No doubt. We all do." His expression turned serious. He dumped a shovel of ash into the bucket.

Amanda picked up the bucket, ready to take it outside when Kari opened the back door. Buck rushed in, brushed against her, and bumped the bucket hard enough that she lost her grip. The bucket fell, spreading ash on the floor. A dusty burned-wood smelling haze filled the air.

Her eyes watered, her nose itched. She sneezed, then coughed and shouted, "Damn!" She heard Wade cough through her coughing fit. At the same time, a knock sounded on the open back door.

"Hello! Anyone home?"

"Mom, we've company!" Kari shouted from on the bench where she struggled to take off her boots.

She heard Wade mutter a curse. "Rodney? In here."

"You on fire?"

"No. Dropped a bucket of ash. Everything is fine. Come in," Wade answered his brother.

The haze was settling in a fine coat of dust onto every surface in the kitchen. Rodney laughed and came into the kitchen. He carried a bag and an extra coat. "What a mess!" He gave Wade a hug that Wade returned.

"What are you doing here?" Wade asked.

"Sheriff called. Said we could find you out here."

Someone entered behind Rodney. Amanda recognized Wade's ex-fiancée and groaned. She wiped a dirty hand across her face before realizing she was as covered in ash as Wade.

Melissa made a face at her surroundings. "Oh, Wade! How awful for you. We've all been so worried. I had to come with Rodney to make sure you were all right. We've come to take you home. You're covered in ash."

Wade looked at Rodney, who shrugged. Then Wade looked at Amanda with an apologetic expression. Melissa was too busy making sure nothing touched her beautifully tailored coat and that her boots missed the gray puddles from the snow and ice Rodney's boots had tracked across the floor.

"I brought you clothes and a jacket," Rodney said. "I can't tell you how worried I was when the cops called and said they found your car, or the relief when the sheriff called last night. I'd have come sooner, but he reassured me you were safe."

Amanda walked to the back door landing as Rodney talked. She picked Kari up and carried her through the kitchen to the staircase in the living room. Kari clutched her, her eyes wary with the strangers' entry. Placing her daughter on the bottom step, she whispered. "Go upstairs, pumpkin, and play in your bedroom until I get this mess cleaned up."

"Does Mr. Preston have to go home?" Kari asked in as low a voice.

"Yes, honey. He does."

"Will we see him again?"

"Of course you will," Wade said, startling Amanda.

He knelt to be on eye level with Kari. Amanda hadn't heard him follow her. Ash lightly coated his face except for where his skin had creased when he closed his eyes against the haze. His clothes were also coated.

"You and my mommy look funny."

He lightly flicked Kari's nose. "We're covered in ash, so I bet we do. I'm going to tell you good-bye now, okay?"

Kari smiled. "Yes." She hugged Wade, despite his mess, and headed up the stairs.

Wade turned away without saying anything more. He took the bag from Rodney and entered the bathroom off the kitchen.

"I can't tell you how grateful my parents and I are that you found Wade," Rodney said.

"Yes. That was very kind of you," Melissa said. "Just how did he come here anyway?"

"I found him while walking my dog and dragged him home," Amanda said, giving Melissa a slightly satiric smile. She turned to Rodney. "I'm very sorry for the worry you must have endured, but the phone was dead, so I couldn't call you."

"You don't have a cell?" Melissa asked, her voice derisive in disbelief. She was perfectly groomed and wearing a stylish pant set.

The bathroom door closed with a snap. Wade limped into the kitchen frowning. His change of clothes was faster than hers, and he had washed his face. Some ash clung to his hair. He wore zipper boots, one unzipped over his swollen ankle.

"No, I don't. The last person in Manistee without one, I'm sure. Wade seems to have lost his."

"Well, we'll get Wade out of your way," Rodney said.

"I need to help clean up this up," Wade replied. "I really don't know why you came, Melissa,"

"No, you don't, I can handle it," Amanda said looking at Rodney and Melissa.

Rodney held up the coat he had brought and helped Wade into it.

"Because I was worried about you, of course." Melissa finally answered. Her previous sour look transformed with such a heart-warming smile that Amanda was surprised Wade didn't melt. His face remained blank.

Wade ignored Melissa and walked to Amanda. He picked up her hand. "I can't tell you how grateful I am. A simple thanks doesn't seem to cover it, but I do thank you." The squeeze he gave her hand also affected her heart. *Then leave my land alone.* She didn't say the words, only looked him in the eye.

His gaze dropped from hers, and he turned to Rodney. "Help me out to the car."

Rodney nodded at Amanda. "Thanks, Ms. Blanchard, for all you've done for Wade. Goodbye." He offered his arm to Wade. "We'll stop by the medical center on the way home. You can stay at my place. You'll never get up the stairs to your flat."

"There is an elevator," Wade said. "I'll manage." Rodney started arguing.

Melissa didn't spare Amanda a glance as she followed the men out.

Six

Walking to the kitchen window, Amanda pushed the curtain aside and watched Rodney help Wade into the passenger's seat. Somewhere inside her, a part of her already missed him. Melissa said something that Rodney must have negated as she frowned and entered the back seat with a very petulant movement.

"Didn't get to sit in the center between the brothers? Good for you, Rodney. Wade needs more room for his bad ankle. Her blonde hair might be real, but the rest of her is pure fake—uppity, rude bitch." She straightened from leaning over the counter. Looking at her surroundings, she sighed. "I suppose it's a good thing I don't have anything better to do than clean the house."

She vacuumed the kitchen floor and emptied the canister outdoors. It took the rest of the morning to mop the floor and get the cinders and ash dust off every flat surface in the house. If she occasionally muttered to herself, she found no answers to what plagued her. It seemed clear Wade was grateful and willing to be a friend, maybe help her in her dilemma, but he was not interested in her. But then, why should he be? They had nothing in common but one shared storm. Besides, however much she might want it to be different, he wanted to put her and Kari out of their home.

Listening to the radio while she prepared Kari's lunch, she heard the newscast's co-hosts report about Wade's shooting. Then, much to her outrage, they gave information about her. How Wade's firm had offered to purchase her land, how she was delinquent on her taxes and ended with a witness who claimed she had stormed into his office shouting threats. One co-host then speculated about her motives for holding Wade at her house while he was wounded. The other co-host answered, "Who shot Mr. Preston is unclear, but police are investigating."

"Like I did it?" She sliced Kari's sandwich into four squares with a ferocious motion. "Yeah, I planned the snowstorm. Called this poor misguided man into my lair, shot him, and dragged him home while taking care of my daughter and sabotaging the power grid for an electric outage. If I'm that good, I wonder why I didn't finish him off and dispose of the body?"

"Did I do something bad?" Kari asked, pulling Amanda out of her rant.

She felt her face flush and gave Kari a sheepish smile. "No, honey, not you. I'm mad at the world today, and talking to myself about the unfairness of it all. Did I scare you?"

"You always talk to the air when you're mad. Is it because Mr. Preston left?"

Amanda looked at Kari. "Yes. I kind of liked having him here."

"Me too. Is he coming back?"

"No, I don't think so. He was only here because of the storm." She gave Kari a hug. "It's okay, though, because I have you and you have me, right?"

"Yep. I cleaned up my house, too," Kari said.

"You want to watch a video?" Amanda asked as the phone rang.

"No. I'm going to play upstairs in my house." Kari went upstairs as Amanda answered the phone.

"I find what you have done disgusting." An older woman's loud, accusing voice erupted from the speaker. An abrupt click and dial tone followed before Amanda could squeak one word. She clenched her jaw at the unfair attack and the abrupt, cowardly hang-up, but there was nothing to do but ignore the call. It was only the first of many that disrupted her work. She finally took the phone off the hook.

She felt sticky with grime as she put the cleaning equipment away. Her body ached from her exertions. At least the house was clean.

She heard Lark calling from the back door. Amanda sighed. *Who could have guessed I'd have so many calls and visitors in one day? Bad Karma attracting more disaster?*

"Come on in. I'll be down in a sec," Amanda called to her friend, hearing the chatter of Lark's two little boys. Reaching the door to the back door landing, she watched Lark unbutton her coat while Lark watched Rick and Jack, who sat on the bench tugging off their boots. "Frank's working," she said, too loudly, "pulling overtime with the aftereffects of the storm," she shouted as she hung up the coats.

"Hi," Amanda said from the door into the living room. "Quit yelling. I'm right here."

Lark spun around. One sight of Amanda and she gasped, "Oh my God, you're a mess. What happened?"

Jack, the older boy, asked, "Where's Kari?"

"In her room."

"Is she being punished?" Rick asked.

Amanda smiled. "No. She's playing in the playhouse her Grandma Gayle gave her."

Both boys scooted by her, and she heard their feet stomping up the stairs.

"That ought to keep them busy for a while," Lark said. "So what happened? You and Preston get into a fight?" She laughed.

Amanda whipped her hands through her hair. "No. I dumped ash while emptying the stove. Buck bumped the pail and I lost my balance. The contents went all over everything. I've just finished cleaning up the mess. Make some fresh coffee while I take a shower."

Lark nodded. "Will do. I brought supper. The roads are slippery with all the slush. Thought you might be low on fixins."

Amanda grinned. Only Lark would think that. "I'm only a few miles from town, not out in the boondocks, and I do try to keep the pantry full, but thanks anyway. I think I'm too tired to make dinner. What time is it?"

"A few minutes after three, but I'm only leaving supper, not staying...or at least only staying long enough to hear your story. Anything heard on the news has to be better in person." She walked to the kitchen sink, motioning Amanda away with her fingers. "For heaven's sake, go shower."

Looking in the bathroom mirror, Amanda groaned. She was a mess, her face smudged with gray, hair lined with ash. Her eyes were bloodshot, and she looked haggard. Remembering Melissa's perfect grooming, she grimaced. What a comparison for Wade. *No wonder he couldn't maintain eye contact with me. He was probably choking, trying not to laugh out loud!* She turned on the shower and pulled off her clothes while the hot water came through the pipes.

"Nonsense! Don't be so foolish" she admonished herself. "He couldn't care less."

She quickly turned away from the mirror and shoved the dirty clothes in the hamper. The hot water finally reached the showerhead. She stepped into the tub, reveling in the delightful stream of wet heat pelting her tired muscles and cascading over her skin. She washed her hair three times.

Pushing the faucet control off, she wrapped one towel around her body and another around her wet hair, then headed for her bedroom.

Before going downstairs, she listened to the children's chatter for a minute. Kari, Jack, and Rick were playing inside the cardboard construction painted like a house. Jack, as oldest, bossed the other two.

A few seconds later, she entered the kitchen. Lark had made tea rather than coffee. She looked up from a magazine as Amanda entered. "Feel better?"

"Yes. Much. Clean is good. Kids are playing quietly. Jack is pretending to be a teacher."

"Quietly? That's a change. They love that cardboard house." Lark grinned. "I'll pour you some tea."

"Okay. Thank you. Shouldn't I be playing hostess?" Amanda asked as she sat.

"You're excused because of special circumstances." Placing the mug in front of Amanda, she smiled. "Okay. Tell me about your adventure."

Amanda glanced at Lark. "Shouldn't you be at work?"

"I was at work this morning, but by noon decided I had to see you."

"Curiosity?"

"Absolutely. What good is having your best friend involved in the biggest news story around Manistee if you don't know the whole story? So give."

Smiling, Amanda described how she had found Wade, interrupted by Lark's horrified exclamations and funny snide quips.

Lark huffed with a displeased expression, the brown layers of her superbly cut hair sliding back and forth as she talked with accompanying hand motions, refilled their cups, or shook her head.

"What was he doing on the back of your property?"

"I don't know, lost, I guess. His car was about a mile away."

"You sure he wasn't surveying? There are other houses on the road closer than yours he could have gone to in an emergency."

Amanda laughed. "Not if he was lost in a storm like that one. And I didn't find any equipment. If he didn't stay on the road, he would have possibly gotten onto my property first. I think he was pretty dazed from the accident."

Lark's mouth firmed in indignation. "The evidence could be under the snow." She took a sip of tea as she glanced at Amanda. Putting her cup down, she said, "Just joking. Frank didn't tell me much, dratted man. Clammed up because of possible work-related information. So tell me the rest. What does he look like naked?"

"Lark!" Amanda protested and laughed. She let her smile tell the story.

"Better than Grant?"

"Way better. Gorgeous."

"Bigger?"

"In every way."

"When did he leave?"

"His brother Rodney picked him up this morning; with his ex, maybe not so ex, fiancée tagging along."

"Melissa came with Rodney?" Lark's expression became speculative. "I had heard they'd broken off the engagement months ago."

"That's what Wade claimed."

"Strange. I wouldn't keep pushing myself into a man's presence if he told me no marriage, no way, no how. I wonder how adamant he was."

"Or how relentless she is. I had the same thoughts. So either he didn't break it off as he said, or Melissa just won't accept no. After spending time with Wade, I tend to believe him."

"Don't. He is obviously trying to get you to like him so he can finagle you into selling your land. You don't want him, do you?"

"I like Wade." Amanda closed her eyes and imagined how he had looked at breakfast. "But I might be suffering remnants of an unrequited adolescent hormone-driven pipedream." *Like her hormones were in charge now?*

"We all liked him back then." Lark's face took on a dreamy look. "What wasn't to like? He was—and is—very handsome."

Amanda sighed. "These last few days he acted differently from how I suspected he would behave. I mean, once I was sure he was going to live. He never demanded anything, helped as much as he could, and seemed to genuinely like Kari. She enjoyed the attention he gave her, too."

Lark huffed. "And that has affected your good sense? He never said he wasn't after your land, did he?"

"No, he didn't."

"Did he look at you with anything other than friendliness? Did he come on to you? Besides, it doesn't look like Melissa is much of an 'ex' fiancée, anyhow. Otherwise, she wouldn't have come, would she? And getting between two participants in a break-up situation isn't smart. Probably some small argument they will patch up and move on into wedded bliss and good-luck to Wade."

"You're probably right," Amanda replied, trying to sound chipper, but the thought dismayed and hurt.

Lark told her own story of the storm and her adventure at being caught in the house with two rowdy boys. "I think I'm glad to be a working mother."

Her friend's brusque manner was so typical of the conversations they frequently enjoyed Amanda felt her tension drain away. They were soon laughing. The situation felt wonderfully normal after the last few days.

She finally added, "Grant called."

Lark's eye's widened. "What? Why didn't you tell me that earlier?"

"Because he doesn't matter. I hung up on him. You know that after paying the divorce settlement, I've been short on cash?"

Lark swore. "I know everything the bum took, including cleaning out your savings. Plus, you had to sell off the acreage to pay him. Don't tell me he expects more?"

"It seems news of my impending profit from the sale of my house has reached him."

"And he wants what—to try to woo you into giving him more money out of the goodness of your heart? Or did he think you ought to get back together?"

"I'm not sure. I have to guess, but he probably knows I'm late on the taxes and wants to offer good advice about selling.

"He was always full of shit. You're worried about the taxes?"

Amanda shrugged. "I have a year to pay them off, but the property values around here have risen so much with all the development. When the letter came from Preston's company, I went ballistic and stormed off to confront him."

"Yeah, you told me that. Served the jerk right."

"That's all I did, I swear it! I did not shoot him, or try to force him off the road, and I did not threaten to harm him at his office. I only went out the night of the storm because Noona was loose. I was worried about her foaling. She is very close."

"Of course you had to find her. A good foal could possibly pay your back taxes. It is a good plan, Amanda. Noona has fine bloodlines, and when you and your dad were showing her, she did great in the ring."

"She did, didn't she?" Amanda smiled, but it felt lopsided. "I pulled Wade back to the house, but when I got him safely inside, the phone was out, and then the electricity failed. I was too busy trying to save his life and keep us all warm to think of anything else. End of story. Except for what the news is reporting."

"News, smooze. Those two clowns aren't the news, just drive entertainment. The station has been telling that story since early morning drive time, so I'm wondering who gave them the information. You kept Wade alive," Lark said. "That's what counts. Did Wade have any idea who shot him? That was all anyone was talking about at the shop this morning, and you can't imagine the number of women who made their appointments. Of course, town was pretty well plowed by then. You'd laugh at all the speculation, but that's all it is, Amanda, gossip."

"Wade had hoped to keep the situation a secret."

"Once Frank made his report, it was out of his hands," Lark said. Her gaze searched Amanda.

Amanda looked at her cup and took a sip of the cold liquid. "Wade said he didn't see who it was. You know how snow blows up when a truck passes you during a storm. Slush hitting your windshield blinds you."

Lark nodded. "Only it wasn't slush but a bullet. Frank says they found a truck on the roadside, and I heard on my police scanner it was registered to Bruce Kelder, who had reported it stolen. You won't believe this..."

"Lark..."

"I'm not saying anything more than what's already public knowledge, not anything I heard from Frank. Well, I did hear a bit more from him, but not the part I am about to tell you. He wouldn't tell me anything really important about an investigation, anyhow."

"Which is why you had to come here today?"

"Exactly. All I've heard is gossip and rumor." She rolled her eyes and looked at Amanda. "Frank told me about the truck, yes, but he knows I would never tell anyone anything. Except you, of course."

Amanda grinned. "Of course. But then, Frank doesn't know who I'd tell, does he?"

"Well, no, but anyway, rumor has it that Bruce was Melissa's old boyfriend during her wild teenage years in East Grand Rapids."

"You know better than to believe everything you hear," Amanda said.

"Well, everyone knows you are my best friend, so if they knew anything about the situation, they told me." Lark smiled. "I must admit everyone who wanted to know about any connection between Wade and you, made their appointment."

"There is no connection other than his company wants my land, and I found him collapsed in my orchard during the storm, or rather, Buck did."

Amanda sighed, too. This was not the first time her name had been bandied about Lark's shop. Her marriage, Marla's accident that killed both her and Kari's father, her adoption of Kari, and Grant's desertion had been duly and thoroughly discussed. Lark had disclosed to Amanda everything she heard and all she said.

"One of my clients said Melissa claimed you probably shot Wade. That you were so infuriated when you went into his office that afternoon, it was probably a crime of passion."

"I was at his office, and Melissa was very provocative. I can't remember exactly what I said, except I'd fight Wade's plans."

"Frank said Wade confirmed you never threatened him."

"That's a relief." A brief pleasure lightened Amanda's mood at the thought of Wade defending her reputation.

"What are you smiling about?" Lark demanded.

Amanda grinned. "At least he had the courtesy to back my claims."

Lark frowned. "You think he said it out of a sense of obligation for saving his life?"

"He doesn't owe me for that! Lord, I'd have helped Grant if I found him all but dead in my orchard."

Lark giggled. "Bet you'd have had to think twice about it."

"Probably, but I'd do it. But, if my saving Wade's life makes him leave my property out of his plans, all the better for me."

"Doubt that, too," Lark said, leaning toward her. "Watch your step and be careful."

"Careful about what?" Amanda asked, raising her brows.

"Your name has been mixed up in Wade's business, so it's best if you keep a low profile. Stay alert about your own safety, and Kari's."

Amanda straightened in her seat. "You think Kari might be in danger?"

"I'm not saying either of you is. It only makes sense to take a few precautions."

"Why? I had nothing to do with the attack." Amanda heard the panic in her voice.

Lark frowned, placing her hand over Amanda's. "Frank said the police have a few suspects, but no proof. The truck was reported stolen before the incident. The interior had been wiped clean, no weapon was found inside, and the truck was parked miles away from where the attack took place. It might not be the same truck at all, as Wade couldn't give any identification except a blur of blue or gray."

Amanda forced herself to relax, tried to pull the cramp out from between her shoulders. "He either doesn't know or is protecting someone."

"Everyone who saw his car knew there was a gun involved. Frank reported Wade's injury when he returned to the office and spoke with the sheriff. Doc Meyers was obligated under the law to make his report. It was the sheriff's decision to contact Wade's family and release details to the press."

"You seriously think someone might take revenge on me or Kari?" Amanda asked.

"Depends on the perp." Using Frank's police lingo after years of marriage, Lark went on with her speculations, her forehead creased in concentration. "It could be someone mentally unhinged, or someone with a reason to hate Wade." She grasped Amanda's hand tighter. "I'm not trying to frighten you, and I don't see why anyone would do anything to you or Kari. I'm only saying you need to be careful until whoever went after Wade is taken into custody." She dug in her pullover's pocket and pulled out a cell phone she handed Amanda. "Frank bought it. Pre-paid. Know how to use it?"

"No. What precautions should I take? And is this your or Frank's suggestion?"

"Frank's. He tells me the same litany every time I go to Grand Rapids alone. Stay aware of where you are, and who is around you. Keep the phone handy and pepper spray ready. I'll show you how to use the phone. Frank has already put in emergency numbers for you. Keep your doors locked at night, and keep the shades down in the room you are in. Call and tell me when you are about to leave the house and work—you know, take standard precautions."

Amanda sighed. "Okay, but this sounds like overkill. After all, this situation is not a crime family thing, is it? So I should only take ordinary precautions, right?" She looked at Lark. "I promise to do everything I can, but I'm also going to call Gayle and Vic. Gayle is going to California to see Dad's sister. Since Aunt Mary and Uncle Ted are Kari's real grandparents, once I explain the situation, I think they will take Kari along for their trip. Now that I'm planning it, I wonder why I didn't think of it before. This is a good opportunity for Kari to visit her grandparents."

"Why don't you go, too?" Lark asked with worry clear in her honey-brown eyes.

Amanda straightened her shoulders. "I need to stay and work. I am not going to let anyone scare me off my land. I must be at the next planning commission meeting. So tell me the whole scoop from your shop. Who said what?"

Lark's lips firmed. "Old busy-body Brown said that you probably shot him, then you became frightened at the consequences of your insane actions and decided to save him...and yourself. Then the weather interfered."

"What garbage...did I take Kari with me on this nefarious mission or leave her home alone while I carried out my murderous intentions?"

Lark sighed. "Don't worry. I set a few ears on fire when I heard that bit of nonsense. Probably lost a customer, too."

Amanda put a hand over Lark's. "I'm sorry."

Lark huffed. "Not to worry. Love gossip. But not outright lies."

Amanda tried not to laugh.

"It's not funny." Lark touched the teapot, picked it up, and rose. "Be safe..."

"I don't believe Wade's problems are related to me. If he's not here, I don't believe there is any danger to me or Kari."

After a brief silence, Lark asked, "What about Grant? Would he try anything if he thought he could gain something?"

Sighing, Amanda said, "If he heard I might make some money off the sale of the land? I'm sure he would want a handout. He always claimed the settlement was unfair."

"You're not going to…"

"Absolutely not! He got his undeserved share a year ago."

"If he comes around to bother you, get a restraining order," Lark said, pragmatic once more.

Amanda smiled. "He isn't going to get anything. Grant never threatened me physically. He'll go away as soon as he knows there is nothing in it for him."

"Did you tell him that?" Lark asked with one raised brow.

"No. I told you, I hung up on him."

"You've had your life insurance changed and his name removed from all your legal documents?" Lark asked.

"Definitely. If I croak, he gets nothing."

"Good." Lark huffed. "Not that you might croak. Only that Grant gets nothing. Do you want more tea?"

"No." Amanda laughed. "If I ever think about getting married again, I'll let you vet my choice."

Lark wore a seraphic smile. "Good decision. I'll go round up my boys." She placed the teapot on the sink counter and left.

Amanda smiled and picked up the teacups to take them to the sink. She paused as she rose. The situation did not feel good.

Once Lark and the boys left, she called her stepmother. Gayle and Vic must have been out, so Amanda left a message. When the phone rang a little later, she assumed it was Gayle calling back. She answered with a cheery "hello," but no voice answered. "Hello?" The line disconnected. Only the dial tone answered her.

"Stupid pranksters," she muttered, but the call unsettled her.

Seven

Inside the Wee Care Day Center, Amanda listened to Kay while trying to calm her jitters about leaving Kari.

"We only release children to the names on our list. You know that, Amanda, and we never let unauthorized visitors into the children's rooms. Don't worry. If anything unusual happens, I'll call you." Kay sounded reassuring, but Amanda sensed a hint of worry. She felt worried over Kari's safety, too.

"Thanks, Kay. I wanted you to know there might be a situation, what with all the speculation about Wade Preston being shot and with the police finding him stranded at my place during the storm." Amanda had taken a few minutes to speak with Kay after walking Kari to her group. "I guess I wanted reassurance that Kari would be safe."

Kay tsked. "And all for doing no more than what any good Samaritan would do. If Mr. Preston had been left outside during that storm, wounded, well, he wouldn't have survived."

"Since the shooting was reported on TV, everyone and everything to do with the event seems to spawn gossip. People called me, can you believe it, just to tell me what they think, anonymously, of course. I'm afraid many in the community don't think I was only an uninvolved Samaritan. Thanks, Kay, see you tonight."

Later, at her office, Amanda tried, along with her boss, to deal with the waiting room filled with last-minute, walk-in clients wanting to file their taxes before the looming deadline. All her regular clients' tax forms were already completed and filed, but losing the last three days would make the hours until April fifteenth frantic. Trying not to worry about it, she immersed herself with the current last-minute client, who had a paper bag filled with receipts. About fifteen minutes later, an altercation arose in the reception area, distracting her client from explaining his receipts.

"Tense time of year. Someone sounds angry," he said, surprise evident in his expression.

"Please excuse me for one moment?" As the middle-aged man nodded, she reached the door.

"Taxes are the bane of man, and woman," he added, as a feminine voice rose in demanding insistence.

Amanda found Melissa Rillema demanding to be shown to her office while Nan tried to explain she was with a client. Melissa's slick good looks had not changed, although Amanda felt more able to cope now that she was dressed in business attire instead of covered in fireplace ash.

She glanced at Melissa then Nan. "It's okay, Nan." She read Nan's expression of disapproval but turned to Melissa as Nan returned her attention to her computer. A quick glance showed many of those waiting recognized Melissa and knew about the situation. Damn news reporters.

"Do we have an appointment?" Amanda asked.

Melissa huffed. "None, nothing except Wade."

Aware of the people listening to their conversation, Amanda smiled. "I have nothing to do with Mr. Preston." *Well, not in reality.* She never let her smile falter at the discrepancy she felt. After all, a fantasy did not count, even if he was seldom far from her thoughts.

"You can say that after spending several days with him in that dump you call a house?"

The tone and meaning hit Amanda like a fist to the gut. Wordlessly, she stared at the other woman, whose smirk only grew broader. Anger frizzled through her at the offensiveness. Surely, Melissa wasn't so ignorant or dumb to know that her condescension offended. Which meant she intended her words to be rude, provoking, and cruel.

Hoping Wade might also have seen the cruel ugliness beneath the polished surface beauty, Amanda shed any trace feeling of inferiority. Grimly hanging onto her smile, she refused to add fuel to local gossip with another public display of outrage. She simply said, "Follow me," and walked away.

She led Melissa to the office's small break room. Amanda put every ounce of contempt she felt in her wry smile and lowered her voice as she spoke. "Not only were we both stranded by the storm, but he was also injured. And no matter what transpired in my home, it is none of your business. Especially since Wade told me you two no longer had a future."

Melissa's snooty expression didn't change, but she did lower her tone several notches. "A small tiff is common among most engaged couples. It is nothing. Wade will come back when he realizes we're ideally paired and how deeply I love him. I've come to tell you to stay away from him until we've had a chance to sort out our issues."

Wade had told the truth. Amanda laughed, realizing Melissa had changed her voice so no one in the outer office could overhear her admission of Wade's disinterest. "Ms. Rillema, I assure you, anything between Wade and me is strictly about persuasion—him trying to convince me to sell my land. As for your relationship with him, I am sure he is old enough to make his own decision regarding you, and that is of no interest to me. So do not come into my office to make suggestions or threaten me. This is a place of business, and I must ask you to leave. Now."

Melissa's face tightened, her lips pursed, but she regained control in a manner Amanda found formidable.

"Persuasion is Wade's specialty."

"Unfortunately for him, a talent wasted on me. Besides, I haven't seen or heard from him since he left my house." That admission hurt.

Melissa huffed, but a smile returned to her red lips. She tucked her purse under her arm. "I am sorry to have bothered you at work. You are correct. I should never have come here."

The brittle smile Melissa threw at her would have shattered a hesitant person. "No, you should not have."

"My apologies. I've let my emotions run away with my good sense."

Amanda didn't think she looked very apologetic.

"I will warn you, however, not to interfere," Melissa said. "Any attention from Wade would only be to persuade you and doesn't mean his affections are involved. You should be very careful." She turned on her heel and left.

Amanda poured herself a cup of coffee from the pot. Her hands shook.

"Are you okay?" Nan asked with concern. Amanda hadn't heard her approach.

"Yes. I was only surprised. She dropped by to warn me against seeing Wade. Could you hear us in the reception area?"

"No. I had several files of paper to shred, found some of my pencils needed sharpening, and adjusted the volume on the interoffice music."

Amanda laughed. "Imagine! She's jealous of me."

Nan looked amused. "I find it very imaginable. She's obviously desperate and imagines you and Wade were comfy-cozy during the storm."

"Hah! I was more afraid he might die. It is unbelievable what people think. Between those who believe I shot Wade and arranged to be snowbound with him because I wanted a reward for saving him, or that I arranged a storm to seduce him so I could save my land," she laughed, but her voice cracked, "is frankly, absurd."

Nan put a hand on Amanda's shoulder. "People's imaginations tend to fill in the gaps when they don't know the whole story. Don't let them get to you."

Amanda sighed, wiped her damp eyes, and straightened. "I have to get back to Mr. Moore." She took her bitter coffee and went to her office. A few hours later, she saw her last client. After spending a few minutes straightening her desk and checking her calendar for the next day, Amanda left her office. She popped into the break room to say goodbye to Nan and Brad. They were having their dinner as Brad had client appointments during the evening hours. Luckily, he always considered her duty as a mother to Kari more important than working massive overtime.

She started the car, giving it a little extra gas to keep the engine going, then took a deep breath and drove out of the lot.

After parking at the Wee Care Day Care, Amanda remained in the car long enough to compose her frazzled nerves and tangled emotions. That daylight lingered made her glad. She always became aware of spring's longer daylight at some unnoticed odd moment. It felt good to have daylight at the end of the workday. Winter had passed; maybe her problems would, too. With fresh optimism, she entered the Center.

Kay walked over to her. "A man stopped by to see Kari," she said in a low voice that upped Amanda's anxiety another notch. "A Mr. Al Carlson. Glad you warned me this morning. He claimed to be her uncle on her father's side, had a driver's license from California. I explained we have very strict policies about visitors. I didn't let him see her."

Amanda sucked in a breath. "Her father was a Carlson, but I don't know of any brothers. I wonder who it was and what he was up to? What did he look like?"

"Casually dressed, jeans and jacket; he was good looking, very tan, sun-bleached hair on top, rest dark brown, medium height and build; he wore sunglasses and didn't take them off, so that's all I can tell you."

"Doesn't sound like anyone I know." Could it have been Grant? What would he want with Kari? No, more likely a reporter wanting to use a child for information on the hottest story in Manistee.

She heard Kari squeal and run toward her. She looked at Kay. "Thank you." Kari reached her and she swung her up into her arms and gave her a hug. "Did you have a good day?" Kari nodded. "Ready to go home?"

"Yep. Look at what I made." Kari held up a wildly colored paper. "It's special. For you."

"We painted today," Liz said. "Kari got a few smears on her clothes, but they should wash out."

"What a pretty painting. We'll hang it on the fridge. Sounds like you had fun today." She helped Kari into her coat. Shortly, she buckled Kari into her car seat.

Two blocks down the road, nearing a stoplight, she pushed the brake pedal. It pressed all the way to the floor. She pumped the pedal, but no resistance met her foot. With a sickening sensation, she realized she was going to crash into the car ahead of her.

With no time to stop, she jerked the wheel to the right and pulled her car off the road, missing the car in front of hers by inches. Grabbing the wheel tightly, she grimaced as the car went up and over the low bank of icy snow on the road's edge. On the downside, she stomped on the emergency brake. The car skidded across the icy snow and twirled around. She lurched against her seatbelt as the car came to a stop.

The motion stopped, but not her reeling mind. She inhaled a wheezing breath as her vision stilled. Her arms and hands felt frozen to the steering wheel. Her left foot remained jammed against the emergency brake. She consciously relaxed her muscles. Rational thought returned and with the simultaneous realization it was dark out. "Kari!" She turned to look in the back seat. "Are you all right?"

Kari's face was pale and her eyes glimmered with fright, but she nodded.

Someone pounded on her window. She rolled it down, surprised to find how swiftly dusk had fallen. A flashlight's beam swung into the car.

"You okay, lady?"

Amanda nodded. It was a moment before she could speak. "Yes… the brakes…"

"I was behind you. Saw your brake lights flash, then you went off the road. I've called nine-one-one."

Opening the door, she unbuckled her seat belt and got out. The stranger helped her, gripping her elbow. Her feet sank through a crust of snow. Freezing wet swept into her shoes. Taking a deep breath, she said, "Thank you. I was so afraid I was going to hit the other car." She opened the back door and unbuckled Kari from her booster seat, pulling her from the car and holding and hugging her. Sirens sounded in the distance. In a few minutes, the deafening siren silenced as a police cruiser stopped on the roadside. The flasher's beams turned on and off, creating red and blue reflections on the snow. With Kari safe in her arms, she looked up. Traffic slowed to see what was happening and, seemingly from nowhere, people stood watching. A second police car pulled up.

"Amanda, are you all right?" It was Frank. He approached with fast strides, glancing at the man standing next to her.

"I'm okay," she said, wishing her voice sounded stronger.

Frank stared at her for a moment. He touched Kari's face. "How's my girl? Okay?"

Amanda hugged Kari tighter. "She's fine. I had her in her car seat. It was the sudden stop that startled her."

"You're a witness?" Frank asked the man, who nodded. The other officer was already talking notes about the accident. Frank took his own notes while the man talked.

"I was behind her, saw the brake lights flash, but the car didn't slow. Then, she turned off the road before hitting the car in front of her. The other car drove off. I don't know if they knew what happened."

"The brakes gave out. I couldn't stop fast enough to avoid the car in front of me, so I pulled off the road and used the emergency brake."

Frank watched as the other officer checked under the car using his flashlight. When he straightened up, his face was grim as he rubbed his fingers together, then smelled whatever was on them. He brushed the snow off his pants, pulled his pad out, and told Frank, "Looks like brake fluid."

Frank asked the other driver his name, address, and phone number.

"All right if I leave now?" the man asked.

"Yes." Frank's attention turned to her. "Tell me exactly what happened."

"I'd pulled out from the Wee Care Center after picking Kari up a few minutes before the accident."

Frank turned in the direction. "I can't see the sign. Is that three blocks back?"

"Four. When I'd parked, I'd noticed the brakes felt a little soft, but they were fine this morning."

She watched his hand scribble notes. "Have you had anything to drink?"

"No."

"Will you take a breathalyzer test? You should, to protect yourself and for your insurance company."

"Sure."

"Was Kari distracting you?"

"No. She was quiet."

"Nothing else distracted you? Like being on the phone or doing something else?"

"No, I wasn't on the phone or looking at the scenery or putting on makeup or anything but watching the road." Her voice snapped. She took a deep breath.

Frank ignored her tone and spoke into his radio, asking for a tow truck. Amanda didn't listen to the rest, hugging and reassuring Kari as well as herself. Her legs felt shaky and she wanted to sit down.

Frank took Kari from her. "Come on, get in the cruiser and wait until I'm done. We'll do the breathalyzer for insurance purposes, and I'll take you home."

Another police cruiser came and shortly afterward, the tow truck. She watched the first officer on the scene direct traffic. It felt like forever, but Amanda knew it was only about twenty minutes before Frank climbed behind the wheel and started the car. Within seconds, they were on the road. After a short silence, Frank asked, looking at her in the rearview mirror. "Are you okay?"

From the back seat, she caught Frank's regard in the mirror. He looked concerned. She was lucky her best friend's husband extended his loving care for his wife to her, and glad that Lark had married such a man. *Will I ever find the same contentment?* "Yes, now, thank you. That was a very scary experience."

"How's Kari?"

She looked at Kari, but her daughter had fallen asleep. "Asleep."

"You mind talking?"

"No. What do you want to know?"

"Anything unusual happen today?"

"Everything was normal up until the accident." She frowned in memory. "Except Melissa Rillema visited the office to warn me to stay away from Wade, and some man showed up at Wee Care wanting to see Kari. Kay...the owner, she wouldn't let him. Otherwise, everything was normal for a bookkeeper before tax deadlines."

"That hardly sounds normal, Amanda. Who was the man?"

"I have no idea. Maybe a reporter, who knows?"

"Kay get a name?"

She told him everything Kay had told her. Frank had another question.

"I thought Preston said his engagement was over?"

"Not according to Melissa."

"Lark said Grant called you. Has he returned to town?"

"I don't know. I haven't seen him. I thought about Grant when Kay described the man, but he never wanted anything to do with Kari. I can't imagine him dropping in to see her, pretending to be her uncle."

Frank was silent for a minute. "For safety's sake, I'm going to have your car checked."

"Probably only a mechanical breakdown. Car's old enough. But I did have the brake pads replaced a couple months ago."

"Where?"

She told him. Kari woke and sat up.

"Kari, are you feeling okay?" Amanda asked.

Kari nodded. "I'm okay. How come we're leaving our car?"

"It's broken, honey. That's why we had such a bumpy ride. Uncle Frank is driving us home.

"Oh. Uncle Frank? I made a picture today. Want to see?"

"When we get to your house." He smiled at Amanda in the mirror. "She seems okay."

"We were both shaken up, but settling down now."

"I don't like this, Amanda."

She smiled stiffly. "Me either. But I'll wait to see if it was a mechanical failure before getting hysterical."

"Okay, here we are."

Amanda saw her stepfather's car parked in the drive.

"Look, Kari, Grandpa Vic and Grandma Gayle are here."

Frank parked and helped Kari out of the car, picking her up and carrying her to the house. Kari waved her picture. "See?"

"Not too well...let me take a look at it under the light." He made appropriate comments.

Gayle opened the back door, apron-clad and holding hot pads. The smell of roast beef erupted from the doorway. "Hello, glad you're home, what...?" Her surprise showed as Frank lowered Kari to her feet.

"I'll explain in a minute, Mom. Thanks, Frank. I cannot tell you how glad I was to see you arrive. Say hi to Lark."

"I'll call you tomorrow." Frank nodded at Gayle and strode back to his cruiser, the spotlight aimed at her back door outlining his body. It remained on until she closed the door. She heard his car backing out of the driveway.

Amanda hugged Gayle when she entered the kitchen. "Hi, Mom, hi, Vic!"

Vic had been sitting in the chair by the table as a magazine rested on its surface. He had probably been reading, but Gayle's alarm must have drawn him to the door. He hugged Amanda. "Good to see you. And where is my favorite little girl?"

Kari, having finished pulling off her coat, heard him, squealed and ran to him, shouting, "Grandpa," not bothering to take off her boots. He picked Kari up. After tossing her twice in the air, he hugged her and put her down. "Give your grandma a hug."

Kari ran to her Gayle. "Grandma!"

Gayle bent over and hugged Kari. "I brought you a present. Let's go get it." She led Kari upstairs.

"You're kind of late," Vic said as her mom and Kari left.

"My car...um...broke down. Frank Teigman brought me home."

"Lark's husband?"

"Yes."

Vic huffed. "You should have called. I could have picked you up and brought you home."

"Didn't know you were here yet. You didn't call. I didn't expect you until tomorrow. However, this is a wonderful surprise." Amanda kissed Vic's cheek.

"Gayle wanted to surprise you. The drive from Florida seemed easier this year, less traffic, better traveling. Go get ready for dinner."

Gayle and Kari came back, Kari with a handful of small plastic animals, some in pastel shades, some in brilliant hues.

"You didn't have to make dinner, Mom. Why didn't you call? I could have picked something up in town."

"I wanted to do this." Gayle smiled and hugged her. "You look frazzled."

Amanda laughed. "Thanks. I'm better than I look. It's been an eventful day."

"Well, I hope better than what it has been. I stopped by Lark's to have my hair done. I heard an earful." Gayle stirred one of the pots simmering on the stove, although her expression looked worried.

"Can we talk about this after Kari's in bed?"

Gayle gave her a concerned look. "Sure. Why don't you set the table? This is almost ready."

Later that evening, when Amanda was sure Kari was asleep, she sat at the kitchen table with her mother and Vic. "I need to ask you a favor." She explained the past week's events.

"Frank thinks you are in danger?" Vic asked, his face lined with concern.

"No, he said to take precautions. My main concern is Kari. Mom, you're going to California to visit Aunt Mary. Will you take Kari with you? It's a perfect opportunity for her to meet her other grandparents. And of course, the added benefit is she'll be away from here."

"Of course we will! But why don't you come with us? Then you are away from here, too."

Amanda argued her reasons why she had to stay. Her mom and Vic reluctantly gave in, but Gayle looked troubled. Amanda smiled. "Don't worry."

~ * ~

Brad came by the next morning to drive her to work. He grumbled as she opened the passenger door and slid in. "Don't I pay you enough to buy a decent car?"

She sighed. "I've had some extra expenses the last couple years."

"Yeah. Best thing you ever did was to divorce Grant Carter. Maybe I should have given you a raise then, for showing good sense. You need help? A loan?"

Amanda smiled at her boss. His eyes remained on the road ahead. The morning light caught the silver streaks in his hair. "I'll manage, but thanks."

Later that morning, Frank came into her office. He handed over the keys to her car and told her the repair shop owner said he would have it done by the end of the day. She rose and gave him a hug, ignoring his on-duty formality. "Brad said he'd drive you over. Lark said your mom is taking Kari with her and Vic to California?"

"Yes."

"Care to visit Lark and me for a while?"

Her heart thumped hard at the tone of his voice. "Why? What did you find out?"

"The brakes were tampered with, Amanda. The brake line was punctured. Every time you pressed the pedal, brake fluid leaked. Someone tried to harm you and Kari. Could have killed you."

Her throat felt dry and she plopped into her chair. "Why? I haven't done anything to anyone."

"This started with Wade Preston, but the rage seems to have transferred to you."

"Why? I haven't even heard from Wade."

"Wade left the day before yesterday—as soon as he left his doctor. He told me he had urgent business in Lansing when I interviewed him. His brother was driving him. Can Carter expect anything if something were to happen to you?"

"No. I already told Lark. He stands to gain nothing."

"You're sure?"

"Yes! Absolutely."

"Ross Kingsley was your attorney, wasn't he?"

"Why?"

"I want to talk to him as part of my investigation. I'll get back with you. In the meantime, be extra careful. You have that phone I gave you?" At her nod, he said, "Keep it with you all the time."

~ * ~

For the next few days, her mom tried to convince her to change her mind, but Amanda held firm. She didn't inform them of Frank's visit, or what he had said. Kari was glad to stay home with her grandparents, and Amanda was sure she was safe. Vic spent a lot of time outside walking, working in the barn, or helping Tina with the horses, so Amanda felt reasonably sure no one would lurk around the house. On the fourth morning, she waved them good-bye. She longed to go with them, and missed Kari before they left, but at least knew her daughter was safe and would have a chance to visit with her grandparents. Walking back into the house, she stood in the kitchen. The house felt horribly empty. For the first time, she did not feel safe in her home, but indignation made her sniff. "No one is going to run me off."

She ate a solitary dinner and turned on the television. Her mind scrambled around her problems rather than focusing on the program. A knock on the back door broke her reverie and sent a shiver up her spine. Everyone came to the back door as the front door was out of the way, so that wasn't unusual, but she wasn't expecting anyone. She looked out the kitchen window but couldn't see who stood there. At the second knock, the visitor shouted. "Amanda, it's me, Grant. Open up."

Opening the door, she stood in the middle of the threshold, not allowing Grant entry. "What do you want?"

Grant leaned against the doorjamb. His smile held the same confident cockiness it always had, his cheeky dimples evident in his tanned face. With his fringe of honey-colored hair, he looked like the image of an All-American boy.

"Hi, Amanda." His voice held a repentant note that matched a shy-boy voice. "Bet you wish you had a chain on that door."

Buck squirmed around her legs and ran out the door.

"Everyone knows chains can't keep out squat. What are you doing here?" She folded her arms over her chest.

"I want to talk for a few minutes."

"We have nothing to say to each other."

"I think we do. I want to talk about us. I was stupid, Mandy. I've had plenty of time to think things over, and I miss you."

"The divorce is final, and Kari is my daughter."

Grant made a rueful face. "I'm sure Kari is a wonderful little girl. I didn't think I was ready for children. Like I said, I was stupid."

"You're ready to be a father now?"

"More than ready, eager. I want a chance to see you, to show you how I've changed."

"I've changed, too, Grant. Get off my property."

One quick frown marred his face before his smile renewed. "Let's go out to dinner so we can talk."

"There is nothing I want to hear," she said, starting to close the door.

His hand fell against the door with more strength than she remembered. She felt the anger tense her face muscles. "I'm not interested in renewing a failed relationship."

Grant's eyes thinned in anger and his smile tightened. She knew he was having a hard time remaining calm, but worrying about soothing his hurt feelings, his disappointment, or his temper was not her problem anymore.

"Won't you at least let me talk to you?" His smile eased into a genial spread. "I know someone willing to make you a great offer for your land."

"So do I. Just leave. You've earned your last buck at my expense."

"Anything I receive won't be at your expense."

"Last answer. No."

Exhaling, he nodded, his mouth pinched. "Clear enough, but we have unfinished business." Amanda read stubborn determination in his expression. Keeping her vision glued on Grant's, she said, "Any business between us ended a year ago."

"That is where you're wrong, sweet Mandy. The courts cheated me out of my just due. I've had a year to think about that injustice."

Her voice rose to shrill. "Injustice? You rob me of what my family and I worked hard to accomplish, and you have the gall to call it injustice?" She stepped onto the porch and pushed a finger into his chest. "You bastard! You, you...there isn't a word low enough for you! Get out of here before I call the police!"

He grabbed her hands, throwing his weight against her body, shoving her into the wall next to the door. Her head cracked against the stone, his body jamming and holding her in place. He loomed before her, the good-looking face changing to a hateful mask. "You should be really careful who you call bastard, Mandy. Your dearly departed, saintly cousin knew well enough. Suppose everyone else learned what a tramp she was?"

She pushed against him, twisting to break free. "Let me go."

Buck barked, dancing around near Grant's legs. "Damn dog." He lashed out with a well-aimed foot and kicked the dog away. Buck squealed as the force lifted and threw him several feet away.

Twisting and writhing, trying to slide free of his imprisoning weight, she screamed, swore, yelled, "Let me go!"

"Not yet. You're going to be very sorry if you don't do as I ask." His lips crushed against her lips with bruising intent. He bit her lip.

Cringing with the pain, she kicked but could not break free. Grant laughed and licked up the side of her face. She heard the growl seconds before Grant screamed and freed her. He twisted around. Buck, attached to Grant's right leg by his teeth, growled but didn't let go. He raised an arm to beat off the dog.

"Let him go, Buck!" She yelled as she pushed Grant over the railing. Turning, she scooped up the snow shovel left on the porch and wielded it like a weapon. Buck ran down the steps, barking wildly and circling Grant, but stayed out of reach.

"Last time, Grant. Get out of here. Kari is my daughter, and you know nothing that will hurt her. No one cares who her father was or wasn't."

Grant backed toward his car, his arm violently pointing at her. "You'll be sorry! I'm going to get what's due me one way or another. Any way it goes, whether you sell or get foreclosed, I'll get paid." He stumbled and caught himself. "I tried to be fair and come to you first, but if that snotty brat gets hurt in the process, don't blame me!"

Breathing heavily, she watched until he entered his car and turned to head out the driveway, watched as his headlights disappeared down the road. Trembling with reaction, she leaned the shovel against the porch wall and sank into one of the metal chairs. Buck instantly wiggled at her feet, wagging his tail. "Good boy," she said, petting him, her voice shaky. Her lip hurt. "Let's get in the house and lock the door. No chain, but I do have a good deadbolt."

Eight

"When I made it clear to Grant there wasn't a chance in hell I'd take him back, the truth came out. He thinks I'm coming into a bundle of money and wants his share," Amanda explained to attorney Ron Kingsley over the phone the next morning. "He claims that since the judge gave him less than he deserved, I owe him. With the purchase offer being made, and the chance the county will claim my land for delinquent taxes if I don't sell, he claims he will get paid one way or another."

"Don't worry, Amanda." Ron's calm voice sounded very reassuring over the phone. "There is nothing Grant can do. You did not hide any assets. If he wanted to know the true value of the property, he should have paid for an appraisal. He took what you offered, which was generous, considering what he brought to the marriage. He took the settlement. You both signed the divorce papers. It's done and finished—he can't get another cent from you."

"He said I'd be sorry if I screwed him. I told him to get lost." She amended her comment. "Or words to that effect."

"Did he do anything to threaten you?"

"Yes. I was afraid at the time, but I don't think he'll come back."

"I advise you to take out a restraining order."

Amanda sighed. "You're probably right. I'm not afraid of Grant. He's mostly a blowhard. I wanted assurance he has no further claim on me or my property." She thanked him and put the phone in the cradle on her desk before she sat back in her chair.

"A Carter encounter?" Nan asked. She leaned against the doorjamb to Amanda's office, her gaze observing Amanda's swollen lip. It was clear Nan had overheard. The perils of making calls at work.

"He showed up at the house last night."

Nan sighed. "And laid hands on you? For heaven's sake, Amanda, that is cause for worry! You know you can count on Brad and me if you need help of any kind, don't you?"

She picked up a few file folders she had meant to put away and rose. "Thank you. It's always been important to me that I work my own way out of my messes. You and Brad have already done so much, but I'll keep your offer in mind."

"Sometimes working your way out means you must rely on your friends. Don't let your pride end up hurting you, Amanda."

Amanda smiled. "I won't. How late did you two work?"

"Well, the last client left at ten, but we left the office about midnight. Thank heaven only two more days of this. It's funny how April sixteenth seems like a national holiday to me."

Amanda laughed. "Me, too. Of course, there are late filers."

"But they usually don't come to us."

"True. Since Gayle and Vic took Kari with them, I can stay as late as needed."

"Well, that's good news. I'll tell Brad, and as a favor for a favor, we'll buy you dinner."

"Deal. Now, I'd better start earning that meal."

"Your appointment is here. That's what I came back to tell you."

"We have an intercom."

"Yes, but that doesn't give me an excuse to stretch my legs."

"Nan," Amanda said as Nan walked away. Nan looked back over her shoulder. "Thanks."

Pausing, Nan turned her head to look at Amanda, smiled, and left.

~ * ~

Two days passed in uneventful, but hectic work. Amanda didn't know whether to be worried or pleased, but she missed Kari. She had worked late, finished the last of her clients' tax forms, and helped Brad with the last batch of clients. After her last phone call, she stretched and smiled. Brad stopped as he passed her office with another cup of coffee. Her boss had also worked late to finish tax forms. "This is the end. Tomorrow we fall back into bookkeeping mode."

"I hope that's decaf," Amanda said, noting his coffee.

Brad smiled. "Naw. Need to stay awake tonight. Going home?"

"Yes, it's been a long few days."

"I'm jealous that you're all caught up. The days will get better after tonight's tax deadline."

Amanda laughed. "The joy of all accountants."

"Ain't that the truth." He glanced out her office window behind her and she followed his gaze. The pavement of the parking lot looked dry, but small mounds of winter's accumulated snow remained around the edges. Sand and debris plowed with the snow gave everything a dingy appearance. "It's late. You want me to walk you to your car?"

"No." She looked out her window. "It's barely dusk. My car is right outside the front door. I'll be fine. Manistee isn't mugger headquarters, you know. I've never had reason to worry."

"You need to be careful until the police find out who messed with your brakes."

His words brought a sense of unease she had tried to avoid the past few days. She had never worried before. If Frank were right, she had reason to worry now, but she did not know why. This couldn't be Grant. It wasn't his way. Sneaky, yes, backstabber, yes. Auto mechanic? He could barely check a car's oil, let alone find the brake line.

"I'll watch you from the window," Brad said, but he followed her into the reception room and out to her car despite her protest. He even opened the car door for her. She saw how he scanned the inside as the interior light came on. Precautions she normally took, but now seemed to take on new, dangerous significance.

Letting her climb into her car, Brad closed the door as she strapped on her seat belt. Amanda turned the ignition and rolled the window down. "Thanks, Brad, see you tomorrow."

He waved and moved to the sidewalk lining the front of the offices and stores in the small strip mall. She reversed out of her space. Before rolling the window up, she waved at Brad. He smiled and waved back, then disappeared into his office.

It was late. She looked at the car's clock and decided she did not really want to go home to the empty house. She went to Kmart and walked around, selecting a few items she knew she needed at home plus a bottle of scented bath salts. A night alone deserved an indulgent soak in a hot bath. After leaving Kmart, she pulled into a diner, ordered a drink and a dessert, and drove home.

From the street, the house looked dark, and lacked its usual welcome. The motion light sensed the car's movement and turned on. She parked and released her seat belt, nearly turning around to talk to Kari, missing her chatter and presence. She realized how terribly alone she felt. Sighing, she opened the door. *What was that?*

At the unidentified sound, she stilled, stood a moment listening, her gaze searching the darkness around the house. A soft offshore breeze blew into her face and she heard the tree limbs whisper with the wind. A twig broke somewhere. From inside the house, Buck barked, realizing she was home. He continued barking. *Only your imagination. Or deer. They must be moving, looking for food. They're always hungry at this time of year. Don't let your imagination spook you.*

She grabbed her purse, slammed the car door shut, and walked to the house. With a crack and sizzle, the security light burned out, startling her. Drat! A burnt-out bulb. Something else needing replacement.

It took her eyes a moment to adjust to the dark. Uncomfortable moments filled with a threat that had her head twisting side-to-side, looking for anything suspicious. She felt for the step railing and carefully placed her feet as she climbed. Reaching the door, she shouted, "Quiet, Buck."

She unlocked the door, trying to catch him, but Buck squirmed past her and ran into the dark, barking, increasing her belief deer roamed nearby.

"Buck, Buck! Come!" She continued calling until Buck bounced up the steps, tongue hanging from a mouth that seemed to form a smile.

"Come on," she waved him into the house. Entering, she flipped on the light switch for the kitchen, closed and locked the back door, and turned the deadbolt knob, something she usually did not do. "I must be more spooked than I thought."

The windows rattled with a stronger gust of wind. Buck ran to the living room window, his toenails scratching on the floor in his haste, barking furiously.

"Quiet, Buck." He ignored her. Going to the window, Amanda looked out, but couldn't see anything. For the first time, she felt the distance from her neighbors. The house was too far from everything and everyone. She flipped on the switch, flooding the porch with light. Car headlights passed the front, seeming to travel disembodied down the road and soon disappeared in the distance. Buck quieted his strident barking and whined. He paced the room before returning to look out the window.

"There's nothing there, boy. Go get in your bed," she said, petting his head. Buck whined and she repeated her command. He crept out of the room, his tail drooping between his hind legs, giving her one anguished look before entering the kitchen.

Gathering a pair of sweatpants and a T-shirt, Amanda entered the bathroom, turned on the water, and realized she'd left the bag with the bath salts in the car. "Damn. One second's distraction getting out of the car and you forget everything." She thought about going to the car, but there was nothing that needed refrigerating and she was simply too tired to go back outside. She dumped some Princesses bath gel bought for Kari in the water and watched the bubbles froth under the spigot's jet of water.

Within minutes, she had a couple of candles lit, the radio playing the Blue Lake station's jazz selections, and settled herself in the tub waiting for the water to fill in around her. *Pure heaven.*

~ * ~

She startled awake hours later to an intolerable loud buzz. Beneath the noise, she heard Buck barking down in the kitchen. *The smoke alarm. Kari!* She jumped from her bed. She reached the door before she remembered Kari was with Gayle. Sucking in a needed breath, she propped her head against the wall and put her free hand over her pounding heart. The interminable noise continued. She opened the bedroom door.

The hallway was dark. She flipped the switch, but no lights came on. Crossing to Kari's bedroom, she opened the door. The window shades were up, the windows filled with an unnatural orange-cast light.

"Oh my God!"

At the window, she peered out, her hands over her ears, the overwhelming alarm hammering her hearing. To the left of the window, she saw flames engulfing the front porch roof. Even with the alarm screaming, she heard the crackle of the flames consuming the wood framing and asphalt shingles.

Fire! Call the fire department! She ran back to her room and picked up the phone. As if in a repeating nightmare, there was no dial tone. She threw the phone against the wall. Turned, yelling at the noise, "Shut up! Shut up!"

Anger will get you nowhere, hysteria won't help. Think. Can I save anything? Buck's barks penetrated the loud buzz. Escape!

In the hallway, she rushed down the hall, one hand trailing against the wall. The smell of rancid smoke permeated the air. At the top of the stairs, she stared in horror below. Orange light flickered on the floor. Faint smoke wisps flowed between the eerie light.

Her feet searched for each stair tread on the way down, and her hand trailed the railing. Three steps from the bottom, she could see the room. It looked normal—except for the smoke curling around the edges of the front door. Yellow light filled the small square windows. More unholy light with fast-forming flicks of orange and red filled the front window, like burning acrobats. She stared in terror. *This cannot be real.*

The mind-numbing noise from the alarm ceased, bringing sudden silence. Her ears rang with an internal clamor. Silence and eerily lit darkness fed her fear until it filled the room. Amanda gasped, released her pent-up breath, and heard the sound of the fire. The flame-filled view through the windows captured her horror-struck mind hypnotically. Her first breath choked her. She coughed, wheezed for breath, and tore her gaze from the window. Smoke filled the living room. A thick cloud curled along the ceiling. A current of twisting smoke flowed from the ceiling up the staircase. She crouched, escaping the stream, seeking the relatively smoke-free space between the ceiling and floor.

The front window shattered in a loud crash. The wood surrounding each pane of glass burned violently. A sudden whooshing wind pulled at her. An instant later, the ceiling burst into waves of flame, throwing a wall of hot air at her. Amanda screamed, throwing her arms over her eyes and face. She retreated a few steps back up the staircase, coughing, each breath torture. Dropping her hands to her sides in a quick movement, she looked at the burning hell around her. The drapes and furniture were on fire, the heat coming up the stairs unbearable. *Escape!* Her body didn't move. Fear held her in place. *You must move, now! Get out!*

Terror shook her, but she edged along the wall, moving downward. The heat burned against her face and she feared her pajamas or hair would burst into flame. She stayed close to the wall down the stairs, her hands stretched out before and behind her as she slid along the wall until she found the entrance to the kitchen. Entering, she slammed the old door between the rooms shut. Darkness shrouded the kitchen, but she smelled the smoke filling the space. It wasn't as thick as the other side of the door.

Coughing, she stumbled across the floor in the dark, reaching with her hands. Her hands felt the kitchen counter. Beneath the ringing in her ears, she heard Buck's whines. "Come here, Buck. Come." She held her hand low for him to approach, but he didn't come. Her hand skated along the kitchen counter, fumbled over her keys.

"My purse," she remembered placing her purse there. Phone. Frank insisted she carry the cell phone. She grabbed the bag and searched through it, cursing as she frantically pulled item after item out until her fingers felt and recognized the hard-plastic shape of the phone.

She punched the on button. Its light came on, seeming extraordinarily bright. *Dial 911.* While the call dialed, she slipped her car keys into the pocket of her sweatpants.

A man's voice spoke. "Nine-one-one operator. What's your emergency?"

"Please, my house is on fire, I need help." Her breathless voice sounded hoarse and hysterical. It echoed in her ears.

"Are you on a cell phone?"

"Yes."

"What is your location?"

Amanda told them, adding, "Please come."

"Stay calm. What's your name?" She told him. "Amanda, is anyone inside?"

"Yes. I am. Please send the fire department."

"Can you get out of the building?"

"Yes."

"Leave now. I will stay with you on the line until you are outside and safe."

"Okay." She clutched her purse and shuffled her steps to the stairs, each foot searching for the next step.

His calm voice filled her ear. "Are you out yet?"

"No, but I'm at the back door." Her hands searched for the locks and flipped the knobs. She yanked the door open and staggered into night air heavily scented with smoke. She coughed, her throat and lungs burned. "I'm outside." It was unbelievable. The utter darkness of the kitchen lifted, and she could see in the moonlight shrouded by clouds of rolling smoke.

"Good. Now, Amanda, I want you to move away from the house. The fire department is on its way. Is there a propane tank near the structure?"

"Yes." She started down the porch stairs when she saw Buck's leash hanging from the baluster. Her steps halted. The voice kept speaking. "Move as far away from the building as you can get."

"Oh my God, Buck! Buck's in the house."

"Who is Buck?"

"My dog, I have to get my dog."

"No, Amanda, please keep moving away from the house."

Amanda grabbed the leash and turned back to the door. "I have to get my dog."

She ignored the voice as the man pleaded and ordered her. She dumped her purse on the ground and placed the phone on the low, thick stone porch wall, hearing him speak. "Dispatch to fire rescue, please be advised we have a soul in the house. Repeat, we have a soul in the house." It made her feel like she had entered Dante's inferno.

Inside the back door, she fell, cracking her knees on the first step. Pain laced through her in sharp streaks, but she shouted as she squealed in pain, "Buck! Come Buck!" She crawled up the steps, expecting Buck to meet her. He didn't. Smoke filled the kitchen. She cried and coughed. "Buck, Buck? Where are you, boy?"

She heard a canine whine and knew where he was. She half stood, half crawled over to the wood cookstove, feeling her way with her hands. "Buck? Come on, boy, come here. We have to get out." More whining led her to where he lay crouched against the wall on his bed. He licked her face, lapping up her tears, but she felt the tension in his body. His tail thumped, whacking the floor and wall. "Come on." He wouldn't move. She grasped his collar, snapped on the leash, and backed away, coming to a halt at the end of the leash. Buck only whined, refusing to move.

She pulled, putting her whole body into the effort. Afraid the leash would break, she took a step to grab him by the collar and pulled him away. Buck whined in complaint, but slid off the padded bed while she pleaded, cajoled, and coughed in the darkness. Sweat joined the rivers of tears coating her face. Buck's nails scraped defiance on the floor against the wrench on his collar. He was choking as she dragged the sixty pounds of stiffly sitting dog across the floor. Her knees ached, she was out of breath, and poor Buck was frightened near to death.

At the steps, he suddenly changed, scampering down the stairs and out the door. He tugged her forward as he reached the end of the leash. She stumbled down the stairs, falling, but she managed to crawl out the door. Buck, a darker shadow in the night, stood waiting.

"Stupid dog! Ouch." She rose to her feet, remembered the cell phone and put it to her ear. "Hello?"

"Ma'am, are you okay?" The 911 operator had waited.

She had feared he would have hung up. "Yes."

"Are you out of the house?"

"Yes, both Buck and I are out of the house and leaving the porch."

"The fire department is only minutes away. Get as far away as possible." She heard the sirens in the distance. His previous question floated through her mind. The propane tank. "Oh my God." *Explosive. Ferd. Noona. Would the barn go too?*

"What's the matter? Do not go back into the house."

"No, I won't. I'm going to move the horses to the back pasture." Without thinking, she put the cell phone down and walked to the barn.

She looked at her house. On this side, no fire showed, but on the other side of the roof, flames shot into the air, and the fire haloed the house in a yellow glow. Amanda turned her back to the sight but not before noticing daybreak had begun to form a pale line on the eastern horizon. She had no idea of the time. *What time was it? How long had she slept? When had the fire started? It didn't matter. She had to get to the horses.*

Unwilling to leave Buck, she slipped the leash loop over her wrist. However, she needn't have worried about Buck running off, for once out of the house, he clung to her side, quiet and uneasy. The ground was dark and undefined underfoot, and the fire's acrid smell and crackling sound filled the air. There was no breeze, so the smoke rose high into the night sky. This close to Lake Michigan, the onshore breeze could start anytime.

Opening the barn doors, she slipped inside with Buck at her heels. Ferd and Noona moved nervously in their stalls, snorting in distaste of the air's dangerous odor and strange noise. She flicked the light switch, but nothing worked. Noona whinnied when she sensed

Amanda. There was always a flashlight hanging inside the barn door. Using the light, she made her way down the corridor. Running the light along the wall, she found and grabbed a lead rope. She slid open the nearest stall door. Ferd faced her, sticking his nose out to sniff her. She attached the lead to his halter, rubbed his forehead, and talked soothingly to calm him. When she moved, he backed into his stall, but with a few more encouraging words, he followed her into the corridor. She tied off the lead on one crosstie bracket.

Another loud explosion caused Ferd to start, and squeal. He shied backward, his shoes sliding on the concrete. The lead stretched straight. Ferd backed until he was nearly sitting on his haunches. Amanda threw her body against the corridor wall to stay out of the way of his hooves, knocking her sore knee. "Murphy's Law," she said straining to be calm rather than curse and scream.

"Easy, Ferd, It's okay," she crooned to him as she slid along the wall. Catching the lead, she followed the line to his head, patting his neck and forehead, never stopping her calming chatter. "You're okay. I'm going to get you out of here." He settled, relaxed, took a step forward, relaxing the lead line. The flashlight highlighted the glimmer of white around his eyes.

Noona came easier, accepting Amanda as safety and following her out of the stall. Untying Ferd's lead, she led both horses and dog out the back of the barn, talking softly the whole time. Once moving, the horses remained calm. Buck followed at her heels, having remained unnaturally quiet the whole time she steadied Ferd and Noona. Buck whined now, walking between the horses' legs.

Talking calmly to the uneasy animals, she led them through the corral and to the gate leading to the pasture beyond and let them go. Here the moon's light showed the terrain. A small sense of relief warmed her as Ferd walked three lengths, kicked up his heels, and ran a short distance before stopping to calmly graze the winter brown grass that looked black in the dark.

Red lights flashed on all the fire trucks and surrounding police cruisers pulsed in blue as they entered her drive. Spotlights from the two trucks lit up the house. Black smoke billowed from the far side and quickly blended into the night's darkness. Blazing red cinders skittered upward through the smoke. Flames rose like a huge bonfire, outlining the stone edges of her house.

Her heart clenched with a painful twist, wrenching a strange humming noise from her throat. She put her hand over her mouth. Unheeded tears wet her cheeks and hand. *My house.* From here, she could see the fire department pouring water in arching torrents of spray onto the fire. She walked back with Buck at her heels, watching. Men leaned backward at an unbalanced angle from the hoses, holding for dear life onto the water lines. Others walked around the foundation, carrying axes. Maybe they would stop the fire...save her house.

Black smoke poured from what should have been the front roofline. The far end of the house emanated a bright light. Flames flickered from Kari's bedroom window on the side. As she approached, the stench grew worse and she heard the fire's sounds and more breaking glass. The second-story roof joists and the front porch roof burned.

Like fiery serpent tongues, the flames rose high above the roof, flicking around the top of the stone walls of the house as if the fire were licking its lips. She heard more explosions from inside the house as she approached the track alongside the barn and worried the propane tank might go next. This close, the fire's roar surrounded her. The horrid scent filled her nose and mixed with her fear and sense of loss. It brought on another coughing fit. She froze, mesmerized, wounded in both mind and body.

A flashlight shined over her, blinding her. She blinked and raised her arm over her eyes. The light lowed from her face. "Amanda Blanchard?"

"Yes." A shadowed form approached behind the flashlight's bright projection.

"Officer Smith with the Manistee County Sheriff's Department." The officer spoke. "Are you all right?"

"Yes."

Reaching her, he grabbed her arm and pulled her into a walk, but whatever he said was swallowed by the sound of the fire.

Another police officer joined them as she took a few stumbling steps toward the line of emergency vehicles. "Mrs. Blanchard, was there anyone in the house?" She heard the officer's shouts above the noise.

"No. No one, only me, my dog, and horses in the barn. They're all safe."

"You're limping, are you injured?"

"Only my knee, I fell on the steps."

"There's a medic here, I'll get him to look at it."

Buck whined, twirled around, and sat on her feet. She tried to squat and pet him, but one especially sore knee prevented the movement. She bent down from the waist to comfort him. "It's okay, Buck. You've been such a good boy."

A few minutes later, a man stood next to her saying his name and leading her to the rescue truck. He took care of her knee, checked her breathing, and gave her some oxygen, but she did not register much, her gaze locked on her house. Others came up to her. She answered questions when asked, but barely remembered what was asked or what she answered.

As if in a dream, she watched the fire, saw the wooden drying porch off the side of the house collapse as the fire consumed it. Embers shot outward and upward from the crashing structure, what was left of it. Looking up, the roof joists were thin, skeletal beams, sure to fall any minute. She realized how little the firefighters could do. The pump truck shot water toward the flames, but she heard more glass break, more exploding and crashing noises, and the howl of the fire whipped by the rising wind. Fire consumed her home, but the scene seemed more like a movie. The strange bright light within the dark stone walls became as unreal as everything else that had happened.

Inside the kitchen windows, the shadows of men moved. The smoke of her burning possessions hung pungent and unpleasant in the air, stinging her eyes. Everything she owned. Everything her family had owned for over a hundred years. She wanted to run into the flames and salvage what she could, but the heat pressed against her. Words dried in her throat, and she tasted the bitter wetness streaking down her face as it reached her lips.

Someone's arm wrapped around her shoulders, clasping her to a hard body, startling her. She looked up. *Wade. How?* His eyes were dark with concern.

His coat hung open, one sleeve empty and dangling, his arm caught in a sling held against his chest. Looking down, she saw a dark sock covered one foot.

"My God, what are you doing here?"

He said, "Come on, Amanda, move to safety." With his hand on her shoulder, he gently tugged her down the line of trucks in her driveway. He limped next to her.

Their motion drew attention. An irritated-looking firefighter approached. "Folks, you have to get out of here." He motioned them to the far side of the drive.

"How...You're here?" She gasped, unable to say more, although her feet followed Wade's pull.

"I'm so sorry, Amanda. Frank called me. I was on the way back from Lansing. Rodney drove, but I dropped him off at his place before coming here."

"Frank?"

"Yeah. He's here, too." His eyes scanned the mass of men roaming around her house, stepping over hoses, between vehicles, and along the side of the road. Increasing daylight showed neighbors standing in groups, watching. "Somewhere. Where is Kari?" She heard the sudden terror in his voice. "She wasn't..."

"No! No," she said in a calmer voice. "She's in California with her grandparents."

"Thank God." She heard the fervent thanks in his voice, and fresh tears poured down her cheeks.

"Nothing is right. It's too late," she moaned, then spun on him. "Did you do this?"

"What? No! How can you think that?"

Tears burst from her eyes. She placed a hand over her mouth to stifle the sound of her weeping and hid her face into his coat. His arm tightened. "I'm so sorry," he repeated. "So sorry."

"I don't know what to do." She gasped. It was hard to talk, harder to think.

"Come home with me," he blurted, astounding her with the suggestion.

"No! I'll—I'll get a room somewhere. Or go to Lark's." She cried harder. "How could this happen?"

"I don't know. If I wanted your land, I'd never have burned your house to get it, never endangered you or Kari. Maybe it's only an accident. Faulty wiring. Lots of fires happen in winter, and your home is old. You have insurance, don't you?"

She stiffened, pulled back from Wade and his arm fell from its protective embrace. With his bad ankle, he had to catch his balance with her sudden movement. Wariness and renewed doubt overcame her grief for the moment. Not for a minute did she believe faulty wiring was the cause of the blaze, and his comment about insurance sounded like something a man would say while trying to assuage his own conscience.

"Yes, I have insurance, but that won't replace what is lost. The memories, the history. Everything, everything was in there."

"Not you. Not Kari. And not Buck."

Buck whined hearing his name, and jumped against Wade, unbalancing him.

Amanda caught Wade's arm, holding him steady. He reached down and rubbed Buck's head.

"Amanda? Wade?" Frank walked up to them, nodding once at Wade. "You both need to get further back." His look brooked no refusal.

"I had to make sure the horses were out of the barn, just in case... the propane tank, you know," she said as Wade's hand pulled on her elbow, tugging her away. She slowed her walk to his awkward gait. Frank walked with them on Wade's other side.

"You'll come home with me?" Wade asked. "Turnabout for helping me?"

"Amanda will stay with Lark and me." Something in Frank's voice woke Amanda from the emptiness gripping her. She glanced at Wade. "Thank you, but I'm accepting Frank's invitation."

"As long as you have someplace to go, that's all I'm concerned about." Wade's gaze remained on Frank. "Do you know how the fire started?"

Frank returned the look. His lips twisted in what might have been a smile. "No. But with the other incident, the police will certainly be investigating."

"What other incident?" Wade asked as Amanda gasped.

"You think this fire was set?" Her voice squeaked.

Suspicion took a firmer hold on her as Frank stared at Wade. Of course, he had the means to pay someone to do his dirty work if needed. Was that why he was here? To see if the job was completed? She cast a quick and fleeting glance at his face. *No. No. That wasn't possible.* She could not believe that of him. But might her infatuation make her ignore facts?

"Won't know until the site is investigated," Frank said, "but with everything else that has happened, it seems highly suspicious."

"What else has happened?" Wade asked. "What other incident?" he repeated, his voice taut.

"Someone tampered with the breaks on Amanda's car a few days ago." Amanda saw the assessing look Frank pinned on Wade's face. "She and Kari might have been severely injured. Or killed."

Wade swallowed but said nothing. He placed his hand on her shoulder.

Amanda turned away to see her house, realizing that although embers smoldered, the fire seemed to be out. Portable work lights and spotlights from the fire trucks illuminated the area. It looked like a disaster site. She sniffed and gulped back a sob. *It was a disaster site. Her disaster site.*

It wasn't long before Lark arrived. She threw her arms around Amanda and held her close. "Frank called me. Oh, honey, I'm so sorry. Let's get you home, okay? Hello, Wade."

Lark's arms seemed to be the only strength holding her upright. Amanda continued to look at her house. Artificial light, brighter than the early dawn, illuminated the blackened exterior walls and seemed to disappear into the night sky. Men worked inside the ruin, pouring water on the interior. "My home is gone, Lark."

"I'm sorry. You know what I meant. Come back to our house."

Wade agreed. "Lark's right, Amanda—there is nothing you can accomplish here. The police will tape the house off until the fire is investigated. You need to rest." He nodded at Lark. Together they led her to Lark's car. As she entered the car, Wade took Buck's collar in his uninjured hand. Then he walked around the car to speak through the window to Lark. "Is it all right if I follow you? I'd like to be with her for a little while, if that's all right?"

"That might not be..."

"She was there when I needed someone. I'd like to be there for her."

Lark's voice rose. "No! This is your fault! She saved your life and look what has happened! Your enemies have attacked her...her car... her house. It's all very suspicious, Preston!"

Amanda put a hand on Lark's arm. "Don't. I don't believe he had anything to do with this."

"No, I didn't," Wade said. "But you're right...the person who shot me might have. I want to help Amanda. Can you take Buck? If not, I'll take him."

"My boys love Buck. Put him in the back seat.

Wade opened the back door and let Buck jump in.

While he did, Lark whispered, "Do you want him to come by?"

Amanda closed her eyes, recalling the comfort, the security, she had felt with Wade's arm around her. She did want him to be with her. She nodded. "Yes."

"Do you know the way?" Lark asked Wade.

Amanda didn't hear Wade's response, lost in a maelstrom of thoughts and memories. Lark's voice brought her back to now. "Then follow us."

Buck whined. Amanda turned to look at him, and the big dog crawled over the back of the front seat. She hugged him in her arms. "Sorry, Lark. I'll hold him."

"That's okay, Amanda. He needs comfort."

So did she. Buck didn't even twitch in her arms but licked her face in a trusting fashion. There was nothing anyone could do to put things right. She had never felt so devastated, so hopeless. She put her head against Buck's neck. His presence helped to keep her heart from shaking apart.

"This is a terrible thing to happen, Mandy, but things will work out okay. You can't give up hope."

"I know, Lark. It's such a shock. I don't know what to think, let alone feel." Amanda sat back, wiped her eyes against the sleeve of the jacket someone had wrapped around her. She didn't remember who or when.

Unnoticed, Lark had driven from the house. Amanda petted Buck and watched the passing landscape.

"Use this," Lark said, handing her a tissue. "It'll work better and feel better on your face."

"Thanks." She wiped her eyes and blew her nose. "I feel so alone. I thought I could do everything by myself, took pride in the fact that I provided for Kari and me. Now it's all gone. At least Kari is safe. Thank God I sent her with Gayle." More tears tracked quietly down her face. She was too exhausted to sob.

"You have insurance, don't you?"

"Yes. The house and contents are covered, but that won't replace what I've lost. When you think about your home burning, you always imagine what you would rescue. Right now, I can't remember what was in there." Sudden images of her home flickered in her mind, the furniture and wall decorations, the cabinets filled with china, crystal, bedding, clothing, family treasures, heirlooms of no real value to anyone but her—but to her, they meant the world.

"You have Kari, me, Gayle, and Vic. You have other good friends. Nan and Brad are more than employers, they've always supported you."

"The family Bible. My great-grandmother had written the family names in it. It's gone. Oh! And the family photograph box."

"You don't know if everything burned, and there is no use speculating." Lark stopped the car in front of the slow-rising garage doors. Lark waited for her garage door to finish rising, then drove in and parked. For Amanda, it was like waking up. She hadn't been aware of traveling. She heard tires behind them and turned. Wade's car pulled in behind them.

Lark patted her hand. "Come on, let's go in."

Before she could move, Wade had limped to the side and opened the passenger door. Amanda got out. Wade didn't touch her, which was good. She wasn't sure she wanted anyone touching her right then. Buck whined to get out the door, but one-handed, Wade couldn't catch Buck's collar as the dog leaped from the car and ran down the driveway.

"Buck!" Amanda called, terrified he might run off. She couldn't bear one more loss. Buck came back, and she grabbed his collar. She hugged him, "Good boy. Such a good boy." Buck licked her chin.

"Have you been hurt?" Wade asked.

"I fell, cracked my knee, but I'm okay. They looked at it."

"Rescue?"

"Yes. Rescue looked at it."

Lark waited at the interior door. "Put him in the back yard. It's fenced. I'll send Jack out with water."

They entered the mudroom door and passed on into the kitchen. Lark had painted the walls in a salmon color that was usually warm and welcoming, but now, it oddly reminded Amanda of flames. She closed her eyes briefly. Wade's hand touched hers. He went to the sliding glass doors and took Buck into the yard.

"Sit down. Amanda, would you like coffee, tea, or pop?"

"Diet Coke?"

"Got it. What about you, Wade?" Lark asked as he reentered the house.

"Coffee is fine."

"I only have decaf."

He nodded. "That's fine." He slipped off his long coat and Lark told him to hang it in the mudroom. He wore a suit and tie and looked very dignified. When he finally sat down, his face was drawn with weariness.

"Long drive?" Lark asked.

"Long enough."

Amanda forced herself to join the conversation, struggling for normalcy. "Is your ankle broken?"

"It's in a walking cast, but only a sprain and torn ligaments. Walking is awkward, but otherwise, I'm fine. It's you I'm worried about."

She nearly cried at the concern she saw in his eyes, heard in his tone. "I'm fine, too."

"Sure you are." Clearly, he didn't believe her. "But if you feel up to it, there are some things you should do."

"Such as?"

"First, who is your insurance agent? Let me give him a call and tell him about the fire. Unless you want to handle it."

Amanda looked at Wade's calm expression. She knew the insurance company needed to be called, but didn't want to do anything. Wade wanted to help. "My agent is Wayne Eisener."

Lark was already searching through her phone book. As she read Wade the number, he dialed his cell phone. After a brief talk, he put the phone back in his jacket.

"There will be an adjuster here tomorrow morning with an emergency check for you to at least buy some clothes and find temporary living quarters."

"Amanda is staying with Frank and me until she has a new home," Lark said. "No matter how long that takes."

Wade took Amanda's hand in a warm, comforting clasp. "Do you have your important papers and a list of what was in your house somewhere, like a safe deposit box?"

"No." It made her feel inadequate. Why hadn't she taken that simple precaution?

"You have your purse?"

"No." She tried to think of where it was. "I carried it out of the house but dropped it to rescue Buck. I don't know where it is now."

"Don't worry. Most papers can be replaced. Maybe not everything was lost. Fires are funny that way. We'll go out and search through the house after the fire inspector leaves."

"Can I be there when they are checking the house?"

"Yes. I'll take you," Wade said over Lark's sputtered, "You have a business to run."

"So do you," Wade responded.

"Yes, but I can arrange my time."

Wade glanced at Lark. "I'm sure Amanda will need all the support she can get." His gaze returned to her. "Amanda, you need to call your family and friends and let them know what happened and that you're okay. With all the speculation about my shooting, the fire is sure to be on the news."

Amanda's body jerked as if struck by an electric shock. "Oh my God, Mom and Vic! I have to call them."

<h1 style="text-align:center">Nine</h1>

"You weren't hurt?" were the first words out of Gayle's mouth.

"No, Mom, I'm fine, but the house...well it's bad."

"The house and everything are important, of course, but nothing compared to your life." Gayle's voice choked. "Thank God, Amanda. Thank God." Relief sounded in her voice, too. Amanda explained what had happened. She heard distraught tears in Gayle's questions. In the background, she heard Vic's low voice, muffled as Gayle spoke to him. After that, the call became a repeated sequence of reassurances that Amanda was unharmed. Vic's voice came over the line.

"You come out here, now. I'll have a plane ticket left at the American counter at Gerald Ford Airport."

"No, Vic. Thanks, but I can't. Not now. No one is running me off. It's a matter of principle. Please reassure Mom. I'm very thankful Kari is safe with you."

"You're going to be okay?"

"I'm fine, Vic."

"You want us back there?"

"I'd love you here, but no, I don't want you here yet. Take care of Kari and Gayle for me. The stone house is the only home Kari has known, and Gayle—well she lived there for a long time. It has to hurt them as much as it does me."

"Gayle's right. The house is nothing compared to your well-being. For right now, we'll stay here. Kari's grandparents are thrilled to see her. It was a good thing to let her come, Amanda. Grandma Mary, well, you cannot know what it has meant to her. Be prepared for a very spoiled child. They send their love, too. You take care of yourself, promise?"

"I promise, Vic. The police are investigating, so I'm sure we'll know soon how the fire started."

"You've called your insurance man?"

"Yes, it's all taken care of."

"Good," he said. "Here's Gayle."

"I've been thinking of all the things lost," Gayle lamented. "It's so sad, Amanda, and I'm sure worse for you. Keep your chin up, we'll be back soon."

"Keep a list of what you think of, please, Mom. I might need it for the insurance."

"I'll do that, honey. You take care, okay?"

"Okay. I'm here at Lark and Frank's. So call me if you need me."

After several more minutes of an argument with Gayle about her going out to California, or them returning to Manistee, Wade requested, "Let me talk to her." He held his hand out for the phone. Too tired to argue any longer, she gave him the phone.

"Mrs. Estees? This is Wade Preston. Yes, the man Amanda rescued. Please be assured Amanda is safe." He paused. "No, I don't know who is behind this or if anyone is, but I promise you, if it turns out to be arson, I will find the person responsible. In the meantime, she's safe with Frank and Lark."

They talked a few minutes more while Amanda sank into a well of apathy. Lark's hand on her shoulder disturbed her. "You're dead on your feet."

Amanda felt ready tears spill down her face. "I have to call Tina about the horses."

"I'll call," Wade offered. He pulled a notepad and pen from his pocket and pushed them to her. "Write down her number, and the names of anyone else you want to be contacted."

The list was short: Tina, and Brad and Nan. "Lark knows my other friends." She looked at Lark. "You'll let them know, won't you?"

"Sure will. You go take a shower and get some rest. Come on, I'll loan you another T-shirt and some sweats. Consider the guest room yours for the duration of your stay."

Once in bed, her mind refused to sleep, replaying the fire, tripping over every incident she remembered about the house and its contents. She must have slept, because the next thing she knew, she heard children shouting followed by shushing noises and wondered where she was. Memory caught her and her world caved in. Her house was gone. She rolled over and cried.

~ * ~

Lark stared at her as she entered the living room. "The kids didn't wake you up, did they? How are your knees? You're walking stiffly."

"No, the boys didn't wake me. I was lying there awake." *Feeling sorry for myself.* "Stiff, but the swelling is reduced. I thought it was time to get up. What time is it?"

"A little after eleven. How did you sleep?"

"Once I got to sleep, like a rock. Thank you." *Polite lie.*

"Wade will be here at noon." Lark smiled. "Said he'd bring lunch. I'm beginning to be won over by your man."

"Not my man. You didn't go into work?"

"I'm taking the day off. Don't worry, Amanda. You're not causing me any trouble."

But she did worry, and not only about disrupting Lark's household.

~ * ~

At exactly noon, a knock at the front door announced Wade's arrival. Lark let him in and, while always polite, except when defending her children, husband, or friend, her attitude held a more welcoming tone than Amanda had expected. She noticed he wore jeans and a casual shirt. The sling on his arm was gone, but so was the cane, although he still limped.

"I brought lunch," Wade said, balancing three buckets and a huge paper bag as he carefully stepped inside. The scent of fried chicken wafted from the doorway.

"Wow, three buckets!" Jack, Lark's oldest boy shouted.

Lark took a bucket of chicken and passed one off to Jack.

"Take that to the kitchen." Lark handed the next bucket to Rick with the same order. Then she took the last bucket. "You get the bag," she told Amanda. Amanda looked inside the bag and counted six containers of sides and a box of biscuits.

"How are you?" Wade asked.

Looking up, she realized how close he stood to her. He felt like a wall of comfort, but caution raised a warning. In the beginning, she had felt that way about Grant.

"Fine. I slept a little."

Another knock at the door gained their attention. A man in a business suit and coat stood on the porch. "Amanda Blanchard? I'm from the Muskegon Insurance Office. I'm sorry to hear you've lost your house to fire."

She handed back the bag of sides to Wade and turned her attention to the insurance representative.

"Your local agent called last night, and your carrier has authorized a check to tide you over until a settlement is made." His tone was curt and all business. "This payment covers lodgings and necessities until the final reimbursement."

Amanda assured him his arrival was timely. He asked her a few questions, had her sign some papers, and gave her a check for three thousand dollars. She stared at the check.

"Will you be at the house today?" she asked the insurance representative.

"I'm not an insurance inspector, but your company sent one and he and the fire marshal will inspect the site sometime today."

Amanda thanked the man, who nodded and left. She looked at Wade, who waited, holding the bag of sides.

"Have you heard anything? Has anyone discovered the cause?"

"I spoke with the fire marshal this morning. He believes the fire started near the side porch," Wade said.

"The side porch? But...there's nothing out there that could burn. It's not wired for electricity. My grandmother used it for drying laundry when it rained. I never use it for that anymore. Do you think they will let me be there while they inspect the house?"

Wade gave her a guarded look. "I would certainly think so, if you wish to. You'll probably be restricted from the burn area until the inspectors have finished. Did you have any valuable jewelry in the house?"

"Not really." She thought about her jewelry box. "My engagement ring, although I wouldn't be a bit surprised to learn it wasn't a real diamond."

Wade nodded. "I'll take you shopping this afternoon so you can buy some clothes."

"That's not necessary."

"Yes, it is." He smiled. "And it will do you good. Give you less time to dwell on what has happened."

"You like to shop?"

His mouth twisted in a wry smile. "Only when I have to."

"You don't have to now."

"But you'll need someone to go with you—for safety's sake. I can't stop thinking about your tampered brake line. And Lark would have to take Jack and Rick with her, which would be distracting."

She shared his wry smile. "In that case, I'll make a list." They walked together into Lark's kitchen.

"What took you so long?" Jack asked.

"Jack, mind your manners!" Lark warned, aiming an evil eye at her oldest.

Jack looked abashed, but he and Rick were already at the table choosing chicken. "I want legs," Jack said. "One BBQ and one crispy."

"I bought potato salad, coleslaw, biscuits, baked beans, green beans, and mashed potatoes," Wade said. "What's your choice, Rick?"

"Just chicken," Rick replied.

"Come on, I'm sure your mom wants you to have some vegetables, too. What's your choice, baked beans or green beans?"

"Green beans."

Wade cajoled Rick into mashed potatoes as well and repeated the process with Jack. Lark gave each boy a glass of milk. "All I have for adults is ice tea or pop."

"Ice tea is fine," Wade answered.

"Then sit down and eat," Lark said, "You brought enough for an army."

Wade grinned as he held out a chair for Amanda. "Boys are big eaters."

Lark watched him with squinted eyes as he pulled out a chair and held it for her, but then laughed. "Not bad, Wade."

"I assure you that I am a completely domesticated man, having had to take care of myself for several years. And I know about boys. I once was one." He sank into his chair with a sigh of relief. Amanda thought his ankle must be hurting, despite the walking cast he wore.

After lunch, Lark ordered the boys into the back yard to play with Buck. Rick jumped from his chair to run to the back door. "Can I give Buck some chicken?" Jack asked Amanda. "I bet he'd like it as much as I did."

"As long as you make sure there is no bone," Amanda said. "Take the bones off your plates and he'll be glad to lick right down to the paper. Here, I'll help you." She helped Jack prepare leftovers for Buck, and he took the plate outside. Wade rose. "I'll clean up," he said and cleared the table while Lark put away the leftovers.

Wade asked for another glass of ice tea and sat down. Reaching across the table, he took her hand. "Amanda, I'm really sorry about all the lies and gossip spreading around about my shooting and your rescue of me."

"Not your fault," Amanda said. Her voice reached barely above a whisper.

"I wanted it all kept secret, but I guess I was stupid to think the news wouldn't get out. I never thought anyone would think you were the culprit rather than the heroine of this."

"So what are you going to do about it?" Lark asked, her arms crossed over her chest.

"Like I told Amanda's stepfather last night, make sure she is safe."

Lark smiled, but Amanda felt nothing but empty inside.

~ * ~

From the drive, the house looked like a blackened stone husk. Singed branches on nearby trees outlined it. The roof was gone, and light showed through to the lower floor. A man in dark clothes that looked like a uniform crouched inside the cinder pile that had been the front porch. Tire tracks marred the front lawn in muddy, deep ruts. Taking in the sight as Wade slowed to pull into the driveway, Amanda put her hand over her mouth.

"Steady." Wade parked the car then held her hand until she gathered herself. She saw clear through the windowless rectangles to the exposed far sides of her house. Everything was black. It wasn't a home...not even a house, anymore.

She drew in a deep breath and looked around. Ferd and Noona contentedly munched on a huge pile of hay in the paddock.

She swallowed hard just to speak. "Tina must have been here. The horses are outside."

"Are you ready for this?"

When she nodded, Wade slid out of the car. He walked to the back of the car to wait until she reached him. The fire had melted any remaining snow in the yard. Soot-covered debris lay everywhere. Yellow tape circled the house.

"It looks like the fire inspector is already here," Wade said.

"The man in the front of the house?" Amanda looked at the other car parked in the drive. Sure enough, the fire department logo decorated the side.

"Must be."

Another car slowed and pulled into the drive behind Wade's car. The car bore the sign of her insurance company on the driver's door. The claims inspector joined them. He shook their hands, introduced himself before walking around to the front of the house. She and Wade followed. The fire was less evident there, although all windows were missing glass.

"How come two?"

"The insurance rep explained there would be one from the fire department and one hired by the insurance company."

"Why?"

"Because the cause of the fire has to be determined. If the cause is arson, the payoff will be delayed unless they find strong evidence you had nothing to do with it."

She gasped. "They think I burned my own house?"

"There is always that suspicion."

She watched the two men talk. The fire department inspector showed the claims adjustor something. Then, they walked around the house. Amanda walked to one of the windows. Except for the kitchen wall, all the interior walls and the staircase were gone. The floor was deep with ash, and there was a broken-edged hole into the basement. She identified a few pieces of burnt furniture that somehow escaped becoming ash. She closed her eyes and turned away.

"I'm going to go check on the horses." She ducked through the fence slats and entered the paddock. Noona turned from the far fence and ambled over to her, her stomach swaying with her movement. Ferd followed her. "Still holding on to that baby, huh?" Amanda asked while she swiped her hand along Noona's face and neck and felt her stomach. The skin felt taut, the winter coat thick and shaggy. The foal wasn't moving.

Wade stood outside the fence rubbing Ferd's forehead and neck. "When is she due?"

"Any day. I'm surprised she's gone this long. I'll need to call the vet out."

"Is it safe to leave her here when no one is about?

"It would probably be safer to move her. Mitch Henkins has a stable north of town. I'll see if he can pick her up."

Wade was on his cell phone instantly, leaving a message for someone in his office to get hold of Mitch Henkins and tell him the situation and that Noona and Ferd needed to be moved temporarily.

"What's your vet's name?" Wade asked.

Amanda told him. He spoke into his phone, telling the same person the vet's name and to see how soon he could check Noona out, hopefully this afternoon. Before Amanda could object, he called Tina and told her the horses were being moved and not to worry...his secretary would call her and let her know when, if she wanted to help with the move.

"She can't afford a stable."

"Tell Tina there is no cost for the stabling," Wade said into his phone.

"Thank you," Amanda said. "I can see a cell phone has many advantages."

"I want to help in whatever way I can, Amanda."

She walked to the barn, inspecting the outside. Wade followed her. There didn't seem to be any damage other than the soot covering. Inside, the light switch didn't operate. Seeing her flick the switch, Wade said, "The fire department would have shut off the electric first thing."

She shook her head. "No. When I woke to the smoke alarm, the electricity was already off. No lights. No phone."

He gave her an odd look. "Did you tell that to any of the authorities last night?"

"I—I didn't remember it till now."

The aisle had been swept, the stalls were cleaned, and water filled the buckets. "Tina must have carted water here. Without electricity, there'd be none piped-in." She walked down the aisle and out the back doors into the paddock.

"Ms. Blanchard?" The fire inspector showed up at the barn's back door, but was unwilling to walk through the muck in the fenced area. For a second, Amanda searched his face and felt her soul plummet. Whatever he had to say wasn't good; she saw it in his face. There was nothing good about her house burning down.

She and Wade walked back to talk. "Have they discovered what started the fire?"

"Yes, and we have a problem." He turned and started walking down the barn aisle to the driveway. Amanda and Wade walked with him.

"What is it?" Wade asked.

"The fire started under the porches."

"Under them? How?" Amanda's chest seemed to shrink until it felt too small to contain her heart and lungs. Breathing became difficult.

She looked at Wade, seeking reassurance, but his tight regard focused on the inspector.

"I found a propane torch tank underneath each porch. Someone lighted a torch and threw it there. It would have set fire to the years of accumulated debris before starting to burn the porch flooring. Ms. Blanchard, the insurance company will not make payment on this claim until it has been thoroughly investigated. With your situation recently being broadcast on the news in this area, it puts you in a suspicious position."

"The stone farmhouse is...was...a centennial home. I would never have burned either the house or the contents, many of which have been in here since it was built. I have a good job. I had no reason to burn my house."

"There has been another recent attack against Ms. Blanchard," Wade said. "You can check that with the local sheriff's department. There is no reason to think she started the fire."

They stopped at the back of the house. The insurance inspector stood by his car talking on the phone. Two white bags lay near the trunk of the fire inspector's car. *Evidence?*

The insurance inspector finished his call, entered his car, and left without one glance at her, accusing or otherwise.

"I've reported the fire as arson," the fire inspector said. He picked up one of the bags and showed Amanda the contents. Inside she saw a propane bottle with a torch attached, its blue paint singed, the brass discolored, and rusted chicken wire. "The chicken wire was found near the front porch foundation." The inspector pointed to another bag, "Same as the other bag, but that one was found under the side porch."

"My father placed the chicken wire in the openings of the stone foundation of the porch about ten years ago." The memory sprang to her mind, and her eyes watered. "He stapled the wire to the back of the slats covering the lower portion of the side porch. I remember him doing it. He cussed up a storm at going underneath the porch to work, and at the work itself, but the wire kept raccoons out."

"Whoever threw the torch underneath the porch, punched through the wire. They pulled the wire away and dropped it outside, but it was rusted and broke. It must have caught a glove or sleeve. He showed a piece of fabric attached to the wire. "It never burned. There also appears to be a stain that might be blood."

"Amanda, show the gentlemen your hands," Wade said.

Amanda pulled back her jacket's sleeves and displayed her blemish-free hands palm up and palm down.

The inspector raised his brow, but also wrote a note in his book.

"How long does it take the torch to set the house afire?" Wade asked.

"Someone started the fire in the evening. Like I said, it probably smoldered in the debris under the porch before it reached any burnable structural support."

"I was at my office all day yesterday from eight forty-five until six. I made a couple stops on the way home, one to Kmart, and one to get something to eat. It was dark when I arrived home."

"And what time was that?"

She told him.

"Is there someone who can verify you were at work yesterday?"

"My boss, Brad Olson, and his wife, Nan, were both at the office. April fifteenth is a busy day for accountants and bookkeepers."

"You had lunch there?"

"No, I ran to the Grille and picked up sandwiches for everyone. That was about one." Over the inspector's shoulder, she saw her car. "Wait, I can prove it. In the back seat of my car, there is a Kmart bag. I forgot to take it inside last night. The receipt will be in there."

The inspector nodded while he made notes on a small pad.

"There is one more thing," Wade said. "Ms. Blanchard took a bath and then went to bed. When she awoke to the smoke alarm, neither the electricity nor the phone was working."

The inspector raised noncommittal eyebrows and simply held out a clipboard with papers and a pen to Amanda. She took the clipboard and read the document. She signed the bottom of the second sheet and handed the clipboard back to the inspector. "The matter is in the hands of the police now," he said.

Amanda watched the man walk away and enter his car. She and Wade stood in complete silence. With all the additional trouble, if there ever was a reason for Wade to bail, to snatch back this apparently genuine offer of friendship, even caring, this was it.

Amanda waited. When he said nothing, she walked to the back door opening of her burned-out house. A hole gaped before her. Much of the backside of the house had fallen into the basement, but two tall stone walls rose inside the house, enclosing the kitchen. Walls unknown to her. She'd had no idea they had been there. They had always been covered by plaster for as long as she knew. The door to the kitchen, badly charred, hung open on warped hinges. Outside the kitchen, partially burned boards poked out of the walls where floors and ceilings once spanned the space. Below she saw her furnace, the metal panels blackened and warped. She recognized the water heater. Discolored copper pipes were attached. Lightheaded, she put one hand against the stone wall to steady herself.

Wade looked through the kitchen window. "Did you know those walls were there?"

"Yes, but not that they were stone. They were part of the house, but they appear to have saved the kitchen," she said, wiping at the soot on her hand. She looked in.

"They saved most of your kitchen. They were probably part of the original structure, with the rest of the house built afterward."

The kitchen seemed largely untouched, although there was a hole in the ceiling, and cinders and pieces of wood had fallen into the center of the room. Everything else lay in a sodden mess. The wooden doorjamb into the living room was burned, but the fire, encountering the stone floor and walls, had gone no further, though soot coated everything black. "Those original walls must have held out until the fire department arrived. I dread going in there to see if anything survived."

"You won't have to. I arranged for a service to clean the site. They will sift the ashes to make sure nothing is missed." As he talked, a truck was pulling into the driveway.

She stared at him. "This is going to cost you a lot of money. You know I can't repay you."

His mouth firmed and a look of reproach entered his eyes. "I don't hold my life cheap, Amanda."

Her spirits sank. His words told her he was only helping from a sense of obligation, nothing to do with how he felt about her. Two men approached, and Wade went to greet them, his good arm held out for their clasp. Amanda didn't feel like he owed her anything, but sighed. She would not reject his help, or anyone else's.

After the men described what they were going to accomplish, they asked Amanda if the barn was locked and for keys. "We'll put anything we find in the barn." After a few more minutes, they turned back to their truck.

"Come on, we have some shopping to do," Wade said. He placed a hand under her elbow and urged her forward.

"I didn't burn down my house. I didn't!" It was important for him to believe her.

The grim lines on his face softened and he smiled. "I know you didn't. You were working all day, and I'm sure the Olsons will verify that."

"Yes. And I have a receipt in my car, time and date-stamped from Kmart, as well as one from the place I stopped for dinner. I guess that makes me lucky?"

"Amanda, being alive and Kari being safe makes you lucky."

Amanda sighed and her eyes watered. "Every town gossip is going to be talking about me. It is so awful. There will be those who believe I set the fire."

"Let 'em. We can't change the shop-worn talk some of the gossips make." A sympathetic smile crossed his face. "Come on. You need clothes, and you'll need some for Kari when she gets home."

Ten

The next morning, Amanda helped Lark clear away the remains of breakfast. When Frank entered with another policeman through the mudroom door, her stomach tensed, but she settled at the round kitchen table for a third cup of coffee.

"Amanda, this is Officer Tom Stein."

Stein nodded. He pulled off his officer's cap, his short light brown hair nearly the same color as his tawny face. Without his cap, he looked sterner. She thought his pale blue eyes, while lacking piercing intent, sized her up thoroughly.

Frank had told her before he left earlier that Officer Stein would be arriving to take her statement. She presumed the police wanted to discover if she were guilty of burning down her house. To hide her reaction, she took a few sips of coffee and listened to Lark greet Frank and Officer Stein. From their talk, she assumed Tom was well known by both Frank and Lark. Frank gave her a brief smile, though an otherwise grim-looking expression. "Amanda, I guess you know Tom is here to speak with you."

Officer Stein reached across the table and shook her hand while Lark asked, "How do you like your coffee, Tom? Cream, sugar?"

"Cream and sugar," Stein answered.

"How about you, honey, you want another cup?" Lark asked Frank.

"Yeah. Please."

It was but a moment before the men took careful sips of hot coffee. The light from the sliding doors in the breakfast area caught the steam rising from the cups as the men set them on the table. Amanda's mind blurred those faint wisps of steam with the frightful billows that had flared from her house two nights before. A shiver spread over her back.

"Do you want me here?" Lark asked, drawing Amanda from her inner vision. She nodded, and Lark slid into the chair next to her.

Frank broke the brief silence that followed. "Amanda, as you are a close friend, you know I cannot take your statement, so the department sent Tom to interview you."

Her throat clenched, so Amanda merely nodded.

"Why don't you give me your recollections of the day of the fire, from when you left work," Tom asked. When she finished, he continued. "First off, we have already investigated your whereabouts. Your employers have verified you were in the office except for twenty minutes or so, when you went to pick up lunch. We have shown your photograph at the Grille, and one of the employees identified you as having been there as well. An employee at the Kmart on Highway 31 also recognized your photo. You left work at six o'clock, and one of the store employees remembers seeing you there at approximately six-forty but does not remember when you left. The fire inspector also found your purse outside the house. It had been kicked up against the stones, probably by the firemen, and luckily never burned. He also found a bag with a receipt from Kmart in your car. I gave Frank both the purse and the bag when I came in."

"You say you got home sometime after dark. That was at—" He consulted his notebook, and told her the hour and minute dusk had fallen. "That leaves some time unaccounted for."

She explained about stopping for coffee and dessert, driving around a while, avoiding her empty house. "I felt too edgy to go to bed, so took a bath to unwind. Later, the smoke alarm going off woke me." She remembered her fright. "My initial reaction once I realized what was happening was to dash to get Kari, but then I remembered she's with her grandparents."

"Because of the incident with your car's brakes?" Officer Stein asked.

"Yes," Amanda nodded.

"So you have no real idea when you got home? Or proof of where you went after your dessert."

"No, but I didn't set fire to my house. I was lucky to escape."

Lark put her hand over Amanda's and gave a squeeze of support. Amanda's eyes watered. Amanda met Tom's questioning gaze.

Officer Stein remained impervious to emotion. "Do you have any idea who might have set the fire?"

"No! I don't have any enemies I think would be so vicious. Not even Grant could sink that low. I've never had any trouble of any kind until I found Wade Preston in my orchard."

"Except for your divorce?"

"There wasn't any problem except Grant's greed."

"In your divorce settlement, your former husband received forty acres of your farm."

"Forty more than he deserved," Amanda snapped.

"Were you aware he had sold them?"

"They were on the market before he had clear title, but he was asking for far more than their market value."

"Then you were aware they've been sold?"

"Yes, I knew. Shortly after the settlement, I found myself obsessing about the sale sign. It drove me nuts, but then I heard Kari repeat some of my comments. I decided to let it go as it was over and done with, and I didn't want to set a bad example for Kari. So I've ignored looking or thinking about that acreage. I had heard, though, it had finally sold."

"You've been in a fight with Wade Preston's company."

"Not a fight. I don't want to sell my land." Something clicked in the back of her head, and she sat back in her chair. "Why?" She took a breath. Had Wade bought Grant's acreage? She was oddly cheered she didn't have to call it Grant's land anymore. "Did Preston's company buy my…I mean Grant's acreage?"

He didn't answer her question, instead said, "Frank told me you had heard from your ex-husband, Grant Carter, recently."

"He phoned once, and he came to my home a few nights ago." She explained the situation. "Do you think he might be behind the fire?"

"The department is investigating all potential leads. I think that's all I need for right now."

Amanda read his noncommittal look as meaning she wasn't off the potential arsonist list yet. Tom rose and Frank followed his lead. The two men left the kitchen and rumbles of their conversation filtered back to her ears, but not clear enough to make out what was being said.

"It'll be okay, Amanda. They have to know you couldn't have set that fire," Lark said, hugging her.

"So far, they've done a fine job of making me feel guilty." It took her a few minutes to mull over what she had learned. "Wade had to know his company bought my acreage—that is, Grant's acreage."

Within minutes, Frank returned. "I'm sorry I can't be involved in the investigation, but Tom is a good officer and a thorough investigator. You have nothing to worry about."

Amanda's mind whirled with thoughts of Wade. Something didn't make sense; matter of fact, not much made sense. She needed to see him. She rose. "May I borrow a car? I'll be back in a little while. I need to have a talk with Wade."

"Sure. You want company?" Frank asked, handing over keys to Lark's car.

"No."

"You sure? I'll go with you if Frank's status feels too official," Lark said, exchanging a look with her husband.

"I'm going to find some truth, that's all." She walked out of the kitchen and left the house.

She snagged a parking space in front of Wade's office just as another car pulled out. She remained in Lark's car for a brief moment.

Calm yourself. You need to find answers, and you won't if you fly off the handle. Her self-admonishment did not diminish the seething in her belly. She walked into the office. On her last visit, she hadn't noticed the oversized structural drawings and building photographs on the walls. If those were Wade's work, she could understand why his business was successful. She also hadn't noticed the overstuffed modern couch and chair off to the side on her last visit. A receptionist sat behind the semi-circular desk inside the door.

"Can I help you?"

"I want to see Wade Preston."

"Mr. Preston isn't in the office. Did you have an appointment?" Her look said she doubted it.

"No, but it is urgent that I see him."

"Amanda? Amanda Blanchard?"

Amanda turned toward the masculine voice hailing her. She recognized Edward Van Haitsma walking toward her from the glass-fronted offices in the rear of the area. She had never met or spoken with him and was surprised he recognized her. She had seen his photo a few times in the *Manistee News Advocate*. His smile welcomed her with his blue eyes crinkling at the corners.

"I'm so glad to meet you at last, especially after hearing how you saved Wade's life. I was so sorry to hear about your house. Are you all right? Please come into my office." His arm waved her toward the lighted room.

Amanda didn't try to smile or answer his question. He didn't seem to need answers. "I only came to see Wade. I have some questions I wanted to have answered."

Van Haitsma stopped, his handsome features looking shocked, she guessed, at the rude tone of her anger-infused voice. "Well, Wade's out on one of our sites. If your questions are about our plans in your area, perhaps I can help."

Yes, maybe she needed to see those plans. "Perhaps you can."

She walked next to him to his office while he expressed more sympathy over the loss of her house. He showed her to a plushy upholstered steel-framed chair before taking his seat behind his desk, straightening some folders while apparently searching for another.

"I know you've been reticent about selling and understand how you felt about your home. It was a beautiful structure, but the fire changes everything, doesn't it? I want to show you the sketches and plans for the development. We plan on keeping as many of the orchard trees as possible, you know, as a local landscaping touch. Wade drew the plans and I must say they are spectacular."

"I understand you bought Grant's acreage."

Van Haitsma's head rose from searching of his desk's contents, and he sat back in a leather-upholstered chair. "We had an offer on it."

"Since when?"

"A few months ago. After securing several other parcels necessary to the development, and with assurance from the building board that our plans were approved. We were only waiting for the next meeting for a formal vote on the zoning variance. I thought you might be here about finally selling your acreage."

"I only recently heard those particular acres sold, and I haven't decided what to do with my property."

"I saw your place yesterday, and the house is a total loss, isn't it?" He sat back in his chair, looking stunned.

"The walls are left. Most of the kitchen was saved."

"It didn't look like much else was saved and it would be far more costly to rebuild than to buy new."

She took a breath. "It's true I'll be lucky if a few possessions escaped burning." Her voice choked and she cleared her throat.

Before she could speak, Van Haitsma spoke. "We are offering top dollar for your land. You won't get a better offer."

They both became aware of someone standing in the doorway. A glance showed Wade, his mouth tight and a belligerent set to his jaw.

"The offer is rescinded. Sorry, Amanda, but we're not buying the Blanchard farm."

Amanda only had a glimpse of Van Haitsma's anger as she rose with more speed than elegance, hampered by her stiff knee. "That's fine, I wasn't planning on selling." She pushed by Wade and headed for the front door. She heard Wade and Van Haitsma exchange a few angry words…Ed asked Wade if he had lost his mind, they needed that piece of land, Wade saying they would talk later. Amanda pushed the glass front door out of her way with undue vigor and jerked open the door to Lark's car.

Wade caught up with her as she started the ignition, standing by the driver's door so she could not pull out of the parking space. He had to have moved very fast, even with his bad foot.

"Roll down the window, Amanda."

She did. "You knew you had Grant's acreage, zoning variances, and the board's okay. You've known all along, and it's all been a lie, hasn't it? You weren't on your way to your cabin the night you were shot. You would have been traveling north, not south, but I'm so dense, I believed you. What happened? You've discovered you don't need my acreage after all? You are just like Grant—out for everything you can get." She was so angry she wasn't sure she made sense to herself, let alone Wade, but she knew the last was a cheap shot. It didn't matter. The pain of betrayal fed her fury. "Get out of the way, or I swear I'll run—"

He moved with lightning speed, pulled open her door, grabbed her by the arm, and pulled her out of the car before she finished her threat to run over him. He gave her one second to gain secure footing.

"You're too hysterical to be driving." He pulled the keys from the car and slammed the door. The unexpectedness shocked her. She didn't fight but let him pull her along as he limped to the sidewalk leading around the side of the building toward the river. While deploring his aggressive actions—not even Grant had ever dared to treat her this way, she discovered she wanted to hear what he had to say.

~ * ~

At the rear of the old brick building, he pulled her through a door facing the Manistee River running behind the buildings, then into an elevator next to the staircase leading to the second floor. They didn't speak. Wade rubbed his wounded shoulder, a pained expression on his face. Amanda closed her eyes and took several deep breaths.

She had acted like a fool, letting her emotions overwhelm rational thought. She looked at Wade.

He watched the door, anger etched his face, and maybe pain. He seemed to sense her observation, and aware he still held her arm, he released her. "I'm sorry. I didn't mean to manhandle you." His voice was softer but clipped. "I've been a little stressed."

Why was he angry with her? She was the one who should be angry. Somehow, the thought calmed her, along with his apology.

She nodded. "It's all right. You didn't hurt me. And you're right...I was too angry to drive, safely, at least."

When the elevator door opened upstairs, a breathtaking view of the river showed through a wall of windows. The space was open, modern, and masculine, but the muted colors of the furniture reflected the grays, greens, and blues of the window view.

"My apartment." His hand waved her to the far side of the open space. He hobbled past a sofa arrangement looking out onto the river to reach the far side of the room. Amanda looked around as she followed him. She decided a wall behind a kitchen and dining area must hide a bedroom and bath. Beautiful rugs covered the hardwood floors. A drafting table occupied one section of the room. He led her there. Plans were clamped to the surface. She recognized the lakeshore section, the major roads, but the plan wasn't what she expected.

"This was the original plan Rodney and I drew up for The View Condominiums."

"But..." Amanda frowned and ran her finger over the topographic map. "This only includes a small section of my neighbor's northern acres."

"That's why I was surprised to see the offer my company sent you."

"Your signature was on it. I'm supposed to believe an intelligent businessman like you didn't read the contents of a letter he signed?"

"Yes! I did not sign it!" His voice rose and his face showed how her words stung. "The offer wasn't a legitimate offer from my company." His face reddened. "Or at least, not from me." He slapped the flat of his palm on the paper-covered drafting table. "Your land was only incidental in these plans."

Unasked questions dumbfounded her for a moment. "But Mr. Van Haitsma told me you had options on Grant's acreage, which is on the southern side of my property, nowhere near where your condominiums are planned."

"I know. Ed wanted more land, but Grant accepted another offer."

Eleven

"I don't understand," Amanda said, studying the diagram on the table.

"This project," Wade waved his hand over the blueprint, "isn't scheduled to break ground until next spring. Ed came to me a few months ago and said someone else was bidding on the parcels we wanted. He snooped around and discovered another project slated for this general area. He thought we needed to secure the property as soon as possible. I agreed, but I was up to my ears in finishing another project near the casino, so I told him to use his judgment and do whatever it took to protect the project. This was Rodney's first big assignment. I wanted to make sure it reached completion."

He shrugged. "It seems a bidding war began. Your land is now the only property remaining between these two projects."

"You didn't buy Grant's acreage?"

"Ed had an option on it, but Grant withdrew the option the day of the storm. He hadn't, however, returned the earnest money. Ed protested. Now there seems to be a small legal tangle over who has the right to the purchase."

Wade ran his hands through his hair. "When I talked to Ed after leaving your house, he told me he had made offers on all the property on this project's borders, to make sure we had room for an expansion project that was in the works for a couple years down the road."

"Was?" She raised her head stared at him. He looked both solemn and sincere.

"Yes."

"But you aren't interested in my property now?"

His expression became inscrutable. "No, not now."

Amanda nodded, partly relieved, part...she didn't know what. A thought emerged from chaos. "Who is bidding against you?"

"Rillema Construction."

"Melissa's father?"

"Yes."

"Is this retribution for you ending the engagement?"

Wade looked at the plans under her hand. "Possibly, although Melissa's old man always appeared too smart and civil for any type of underhanded competition." His gaze rose from the plan on the desk and settled on her. "Will you trust me?"

The request threw her. *Trust Wade?* She wanted to, her intuition and her heart told her to, but experience and logic shouted louder. "I don't know."

He stared at her a moment longer, frowned, and looked out the windows. "Perhaps if you knew me better? I mean, you're not angry with me now, are you?"

"No. I'm not angry with you. Right now."

Wade laughed. "That doesn't sound overly encouraging."

"It's not funny. Since this started, you've been shot, my brakes have been tampered with, and I've had to send my daughter away for her safety. My house has been burned, and I'm suspected of arson. After the news about you being found at my place was made public, everyone thinks I'm in a desperate financial situation. Now I'm hanging over a virtual precipice. I believe it is all because of you."

He looked at her with compassion. "I know. I'm sorry. A sad return for saving my life."

"Buck saved your life. He found you. I never would have. I only pulled you into my house and let you warm up."

"And bandaged me. Fed me. Kept me warm. And safe."

"You don't owe me anything except honesty."

He frowned but did not answer, which only told her he had something to hide.

"I need to get back to Lark's." Looking around at the very masculine but beautiful room, she realized how substandard her house must have looked to him. Worse, she recognized her real reason for having allowed him to bring her here. She suffered from the emotions she'd felt in high school. Her gawky, freshman hero worship of the senior star athlete had never really left her, including the heart-throbbing thrill of desire every time he was near. He'd scoff at that the same way he must have been secretly scoffing at her for clinging to an ancient stone farmhouse, only now it was worse. She'd read far too much into his gratitude, and his kindness. Taking a step back, she looked at him, finally acknowledging how far her hero worship had developed, that it had turned into something stronger, more adult, and that her feelings were as useless now as when they had been in high school.

"Thank you for showing me this, but I have to go."

"Amanda, wait, please." He took an ungainly step and nearly tripped as his cast caught against a chair leg. His hand grabbed onto the table to prevent himself from falling. Seeing he was all right, Amanda turned and hurried to the elevator.

"What are you afraid of? Me?" Wade's question followed her.

She stopped and faced him, wanting to say something glib, and though her lips moved, no words emerged. She took a short breath and said, "No, I'm not afraid of you." For some reason, the truth simply poured out of her. "I'm afraid of me, of how you make me feel, of how I believe you. I let my heart rule my head once before and paid dearly for it. I don't know if you're interested in me or just want to be friends, but this time, I know I have to do what is right for Kari as well as for me."

He looked stunned. She turned and left. He caught her as she reached the elevator and stepped inside with her. His hand landed on her shoulder, turning her toward him. Before she could respond, his lips met hers in a demanding kiss that stopped her breath and continued as the elevator descended. As the door opened, his kiss softened, becoming more tentative, appealing in its invitation.

She slid her arm around him, answering his kiss, losing herself in his embrace. Wade pulled away first. "That," he said softly, cupping her cheek in one hand, "was to show you that I am interested. Now, you go think seriously about what it is you really want." He opened the outer door and walked her back to her car without another word.

"You don't want my land?" she asked as he helped her into Lark's car.

"No. Not now. I can promise you it won't become part of any of my business projects."

Amanda frowned at him from within the car. Her heart shouted for joy, but her head warned, *don't trust him*. Grant had grabbed her land and she believed Wade would take it, too, but he no longer wanted it. Grant didn't kiss as well. As if reading her mind, Wade smiled, slapped the top of her car, and limped away.

~ * ~

The next morning, Amanda went to her house or the shell of what had been her house. Pulling into her driveway, she first saw the familiar stone walls, but now they were charred ghosts of what they had been. The sun caught them, but their usual warm, soft, earthy charm was gone, covered in grime. The windows were holes into an empty interior, the gable ends stood roofless, stark angles against the sky. Everything looked cold and grim. The company Wade hired to clean the site had nearly accomplished its work. A large waste dumpster blocked one side of the driveway. Blackened and charred-edged remains of her home filled the box like an ungainly corpse escaping its coffin. The waste that had littered the yard was gone. Small bright yellow daffodils bloomed along the walkway, coming into flower after the fire, although most of the wide swath of flowers and foliage had been trampled down by the recent foot traffic.

They'll come back. They always do.

Leaving her car, she walked around the house, noting the empty windows, so foreign to what she expected to see. The site leader saw her, waved, and walked over. "Hello, Ms. Blanchard. I'm Dick, if you don't remember."

"Hi, Dick, please call me Amanda. We were introduced, I know, but...I didn't remember your name." She barely remembered what he looked like. A big man, perhaps in his late twenties, Dick looked like he had the Dutch ancestry so common in Western Michigan.

Dick smiled a broad grin. "Fires tend to affect my clients' memories that way." He waved his hand at the house and surrounding ground. "We're almost finished. Pete's sifted most of the ash. What we've found is inside the barn." He looked at the stone walls that remained standing. "Those old stonemasons really knew how to make a strong building. It's a shame, a real shame."

Seeing her tears, he suggested they go into the barn, but first led her to the kitchen window. "Most everything we found was in the kitchen. The walls of the kitchen are an earlier structure, which is why you had stone partitions inside the house. Took a skilled man to match the stonework, but if you look close, you'll see the kitchen is slightly different from the rest of the house."

"I've lived here forever, but never noticed the difference. Those walls had been plastered long before my memories began."

"Well, it saved you a few pieces of furniture and some keepsakes. You never know how these rural fires will go. Sometimes nothing is saved, but you were very lucky. We're demolishing what stud walls remained. It was unsafe to leave any of them in place."

"I suppose kids like to explore deserted places like this," Amanda said in a dispirited voice. She looked overhead. The trees were budding out except for the branches affected by the fire's heat. Those blackened stubs looked ugly. She bowed her head. At her feet, snowdrops bloomed amid the remains of burned shrubbery.

"Come look at what's in the barn. You're right, and not only kids, you know, but treasure hunters. Someone's always looking to profit from another person's tragedy. We've got pop in the cooler if you'd like something." He walked her to the barn door.

"No, thanks. I don't think I can swallow anything right now."

He nodded. "Understandable."

Entering the barn, it was strange not to see two horse heads pop out over the stall doors. Amanda took a deep breath to hold back tears. Ferd and Noona were safe. Kari was safe. She could take care of herself. In the barn's main aisle stood the old cookstove. The other appliances were also there, looking much the worse for wear. Looking in one of the stalls, she gasped. The old dish cabinet stood inside.

"Some of the dishes survived, too," Dick said. "Strange, huh?"

Amanda had no idea how long the cabinet had been in the kitchen, but at least from her grandmother's time. It was probably the only piece of wood furniture to survive. She passed the electric stove, her finger coming away covered in greasy soot from touching it.

Dick watched her. "It'll clean up, and so will the refrigerator, but you might want to have the wiring checked."

Plastic draped the backyard picnic table pulled into the barn. It bore a small mountain of unrecognizable lumps. Another draped table stood beyond it with more objects. Dick lifted the plastic. "Saved most of the kitchen, the table's here, chairs are in the stall behind us. Base and wall cabinets in another stall. Lots of soot covering them and some water damage, but they're pretty old, anyway. You might want to modernize with new cabinets."

Did he think rebuilding was feasible? For the first time since the fire, a tiny glimmer of hope began to glow deep inside Amanda's heart.

On top of the table, he indicated a stacked pile of burnt box-like objects and another pile of untouched phone books, note pads, and other books. "We decided not to toss them until you said okay." One thicker volume she recognized as the family Bible. She opened the blackened cover and saw the burnt edges of the pages leaving a feather edge of a series of shorter pages, each less burned than the preceding page. It was sodden with dampness, perhaps savable, but probably not. Odd, the things worth saving were gone, while the phone books, safe in a kitchen drawer, were fine. She looked through the pile in a sudden memory. Picking up a small volume, she recognized her grandmother's journal, incredibly whole and dry. She hugged it to her chest.

"Found that inside the kitchen counter drawers with the phone books and some papers." He showed her the piled papers. "I know a restorer who could possibly save some of these. They probably won't look like they did before, but if they are important..."

"I'd like the name. If he could save the Bible alone, it would be worth the price." She ran her fingers over the Bible's cover, her fingers lingering on the handwriting on the first pages. She looked at the journal. "Strange, I had only been reading this a short time ago."

Next to the books were some pieces of china from the cabinet, pots and pans, the stainless and glasses from the kitchen, strange odds and ends, and the soot-covered china cabinet with the glass in the doors broken. Each ruined item, no matter how prosaic, became a treasure holding memories of a way of life now over.

After a short conversation with Dick, she left the barn. Moments later, she heard him and his crew leave. Emptiness hung heavily upon her.

She stood staring at the burned-out shell of her house. *This is what I have left.* The thought shook her to the soul. She wanted to run away to somewhere sane and safe. Money from the land would allow that. She wished she had a purchase offer from Wade.

She needed to think and knew the best place for that. Turning down the track between the northern and southern orchard sections, she began her favorite walk toward the lake on the back of the property. The apple trees were starting to bloom, the first few tentative petals opening. There had been orchards there as long as she could remember, although pine forest originally covered the land. She heard a motor hum and saw Wyn Poostma spraying the trees. He had performed all the orchard operations since before her father died. She waved, but he didn't see her.

Passing into the rear field, she climbed the grass-covered dune and looked out at Lake Michigan. The breeze from the lake blew her hair away from her face. It brought the familiar lake scent, part decaying fish and waterweeds, the rest crisp, moist air, and sunshine. Overhead, puffy clouds dotted an amazingly blue sky.

The gray-teal-colored water spread to the horizon. Sun glinted on the water. A single boat glided far out from the shoreline, leaving a small wake in white-capped choppy water. She recognized the local Coast Guard station's search and rescue boat.

She owned eighty acres developers wanted for the lake view and all she had done at night was cry herself to sleep or lie awake wondering who meant her harm, waiting for the next shoe to drop. This had to end. It was time to pick herself up and rebuild her life. Kari depended on her. If worse came to worst, if Wade truly didn't want her land, maybe Rillema Construction would. Her ancestors wouldn't mind her doing whatever it took for the family to survive, for her and Kari to be safe.

Turning around, she looked back the way she had come. A sense of exposure, of vulnerability, overcame her. The same feeling as when she had come home the night of the fire. *No one knows where you are, no one can hear you. What were you thinking?* She looked around, searching for anything that seemed threatening, feeling hidden dangers, perhaps someone following her, watching her. She swallowed, her fear frizzling along every nerve. She hated this fear, her lack of trust in anyone, the sense every minute held an unknown threat.

Feeling as if unseen eyes peered at her from some secret hiding place, she ran down the two-track between the orchards. Wyn Poostma was no longer working in the apple trees. She darted back to the barn, closed and latched the doors, then crept to the upper level and carefully peered out the few small, dusty and soot-coated windows, seeing no one.

Stop it! It's only your imagination, one part of her calmed. Another shouted. *The fire wasn't your imagination, or the car, and Wade was shot near here.*

Taking several deep breaths, she closed her eyes and waited, but the panic didn't ease. She no longer felt safe, not here, at home. The sense that someone was hunting her scared her. *Why? Why would anyone want to harm me? Would they harm anyone around me, too? Kari? Lark and my family? Am I safe at work or am I endangering everyone in the office?* She sat in a nearby chair with a broken back spindle, ignoring the thick dust coating it, and cried.

Finally, she forced herself to calm down and examine the old furniture her family had stored there through the generations. Looking around, she decided with a little repair and polish, some of the pieces could be used. There was enough to furnish a small house or trailer. With the insurance check, she could rebuild.

The question remained...here on this property, or somewhere else? Building elsewhere wouldn't be the same as living here, but that didn't mean it couldn't be better.

The police would find her innocent of arson. They had to. Otherwise, she and Kari could end up living here in the barn. The situation seemed untenable. She wanted the investigation over now, her name cleared, the insurance paid so she could plan what to do next.

A car door slammed, startling Amanda from her thoughts.

She jumped up, rushed to the small window. She searched for where the noise might have come from but saw no cars. An engine turned over somewhere, and she heard the vehicle leave.

Twelve

At work the next morning, Nan's inter-office call interrupted Amanda's concentration on balancing a client's books. "Amanda, Mr. And Mrs. Preston and Rodney Preston are here to see you."

It took her a few seconds to respond.

"I'll come out." Puzzled, Amanda rose and walked into the reception area. She recognized Rodney, noting his resemblance to his brother—more boyish and with more finely chiseled angles that made him a little more handsome. He stood talking with Nan, who looked totally charmed. Rodney held a huge bouquet of red roses. Seeing her, he abruptly turned with his lady-killing smile in place. An older couple stood talking with him and Nan. His parents. Wade's parents. Amanda's breath caught briefly as she moved forward to take Mr. Preston's outstretched hand.

"Amanda, how nice to meet you. I'm Robert Preston, and this is my wife, Eileen." With his pleasant voice came the scent of an expensive grooming product.

When Robert Preston released her hand, Eileen's warmer one gently squeezed hers, and her perfume rolled over Amanda. "I've been so anxious to meet you and thank you." She firmed her lips and her eyes glistened. She placed her other hand over the hand that held Amanda's. "Thank you."

Amanda felt her eyes tear. "You're welcome, but there is no need to thank me. I only did what anyone would have done in similar circumstances."

Wade's mother was a petite woman with beautiful gray hair done in a soft, fashionable cut that framed her face. Her suit was a soft muted gray that emphasized her delicate coloring. She wore a pleasant, friendly expression on an ordinary face. Mr. Preston loomed over her, but he was not as tall as either Rodney or Wade. Amanda took an immediate liking to them.

"And we've met." Rodney took her hand as his mother released it. "You're very pretty covered in ash, but beautiful without."

Amanda laughed. "Thank you. That was not one of my better moments. I felt...well, far from elegant."

Rodney's smile charmed. "I know I'm late, but my parents and I wanted to bring you a small thank-you for saving Wade." He held out the roses, at least two dozen of them in a stunning vase.

At the price of roses, hardly a small gesture. "How kind of you all! I'm grateful," she said, accepting the gift, but added, "It really wasn't necessary. This is a lovely vase." It was so heavy it had to be lead crystal, and possibly an antique.

"I found it in Grand Rapids when we took Wade there to have his ankle and shoulder checked," Eileen said, smiling.

Nan rose from behind her desk. "Amanda, let me take those. I'll put them on your desk. Although they would look amazing out here." She took the flowers, sniffing the roses and giving them all a huge smile.

"Thanks, Nan." Amanda turned to her company. "Thank you, Rodney, Mr. and Mrs. Preston. This is unexpected. I've already told Wade I didn't save him. My dog, Buck, found him and barked until I came. If my mare, Noona, hadn't been out, and if I'd never gone to look for her, I would have never found him."

"Then I have to believe an angel guided your steps," Mrs. Preston said.

"We'll have to add a basket of dog bones to your flowers," Rodney said. "And maybe a barrel of oats for the horse. But you pulled him back to the house, so you have to keep the flowers." He laughed. His renewed grin sobered. "We were very sorry to hear about your house. I've always loved stone houses and yours was a gem."

Amanda smiled. Not many had come to sympathize with her. "Thank you. It was a very special house for me."

"Well, the barn is pretty spectacular, as barns go, and it is in really good shape. We're losing so many of our old barns. It's a crime," Robert Preston said.

Amanda smiled at this recognition of her heritage. "The barn has remained in constant use. Until recently, we stabled ten horses."

"Well, if you need any help now, or when you go to rebuild, please call. My sons aren't the only ones with building experience, except mine is more practical. I want to help you," Robert said. His earnest tone and concerned expression seemed genuine.

"Count me in on that," Rodney said. "If you rebuild."

If she rebuilt. Though both men seemed so sincere, Amanda's blood froze. There was a youthful openness about Rodney and a stateliness about his parents that disarmed her. She couldn't truly believe Rodney would either shoot his brother or burn her house. Could she? She decided to answer them with a half-truth. "I haven't made a decision, but I will keep your offer in mind."

Rodney grabbed her hand and his eyes turned luminous with unshed tears. He blinked them clear. "Like I said, you and your dog saved Wade." His lips tightened to contain his emotions. "I can't imagine my life without him. I know he thinks I'm irresponsible and unreliable, but after two days not knowing whether he was alive or not, I decided it was time I made some real changes. So you helped me grow up, too. My parents will appreciate that. I only hope I find as beautiful a guardian angel as Wade did."

Amanda felt heat flood her neck and cheeks. Rodney's comment drew some good-natured kidding from his father, followed by some polite inquiries into her situation. Eileen Preston finally broke things up saying, "We must not keep you from work any longer."

"No, we shouldn't," Robert Preston agreed, "and this meeting would have come sooner, but events have spiraled out of control. We were very concerned for Wade for a few days, even after he left your excellent care at your house during the storm...but we decided we couldn't delay any longer. Please, if we can help you in any way—"

"Thank you," Eileen Preston clasped Amanda's hand and again covered it with her other hand. "Thank you for saving Wade. I..." her eyes shone with deep emotion and she took a few seconds to control herself.

Amanda patted the hand clasping hers and said a polite goodbye.

"Well, that was interesting," Nan said from the back office doorway. "I'm finding it harder and harder to believe Rodney had anything to do with his brother's shooting or the torching of your house."

"I don't know, Nan. I've been fooled before."

Nan huffed. "Grant Carter was a known manipulator before you ever met him. He used others before he used you."

"I know." Amanda sighed. "Grant was kind to me when I needed kindness, and I chose to ignore everything else. The warnings were there. I've paid for my self-deception. I don't want to get fooled or fool myself."

"Trust is hard to regain once destroyed. The roses are gorgeous." She sighed. "I'd like to receive some myself."

"I'll give Brad a hint." Amanda watched the Prestons through the window after they left. Rodney opened the door for Eileen to enter the car and waited while she situated herself in the front passenger seat before closing the door. His father had waited by the driver's door and they shared a few words over the roof of the car before his father took the driver's seat and Rodney entered the back. They must have seen her standing by the office window, for they waved as they drove away. Amanda raised a hand and waved back.

"They seem like very good people." Nan waved with her.

"Yes, they do."

"Didn't offer you a reward or anything patronizing, did they?"

"No. They offered help with the house if I needed it."

"Do you need it?"

"I don't know yet." She sighed. "I haven't decided what to do. Every time I start to plan, I seem to get stuck remembering what I had."

The compassionate expression on Nan's face turned encouraging. "You don't have to make a decision right away. Surely you can wait for Gayle and Vic to get back from California?"

"I might not have a choice. I seem to be under suspicion of arson."

"Nonsense," Nan said with a soft huff. "You know you didn't do it. Neither Brad nor I believe you set the fire, nor do the rest of your friends. You may have been late on your taxes after having to fork out a divorce settlement to Grant, but you weren't desperate, and you had, and have, a good job."

Amanda smiled. "Yes, I do. Thanks, Nan."

"Feeling better?"

"Yes. I better get back to work."

"When are Gayle and Vic coming back?"

"They didn't say. I asked them not to change their plans."

"Uh-oh. You better expect them anytime, then."

The thought cheered Amanda. "I hope so."

"And when you're ready to rebuild, Brad and I will help, too."

~ * ~

At the end of the business day, Amanda walked to her car. A sense of uneasiness assailed her as Grant emerged from the car parked next to hers.

"I don't want to talk with you," Amanda said, unlocking her car, her movements jerky and uncoordinated with her agitation. She opened the door, but Grant was next to her. He must have run around the back of her car.

"Please, Amanda, just listen."

"You can't say anything I want to hear."

"I know, but your situation has changed, and as hard as you might find it to believe, I want to help you." His hand grabbed the edge of her car door, blocking her entry.

"You're right, I don't believe you. Get out of the way, Grant."

"Come on, Amanda. I only want to help."

"How? Can you build me a new house? Get away from my car and stop causing a scene." She tried to return to the office, but he caught her wrist.

"There is no scene, Amanda, unless you make one. There is no one else in the parking lot, and no one on the road will notice anything unusual. I only want to talk to you, and you've refused to answer the messages I've left. And yes, I can help you find the wherewithal to have a new house. I heard Preston rescinded his offer to buy your farm."

She jerked her arm free of his grasp, angered by his persistence. "What? How did you learn that?"

"That's not important," he said. "What is important is that I can offer you good money for it."

She gasped in disbelief, her jaw dropping for a moment before she regained her composure. "You want to purchase my acreage? Over my dead body, Grant!"

Grant frowned. "Be sensible and less emotional. The house is gone, but I know people who are only interested in the land."

"Who? And what's in it for you, Grant?"

He looked uncomfortable for a moment, watching the sparse traffic on Highway 31. "I've been offered a percentage of the sale if I can get you to agree to the purchase."

At her prolonged silence, he finally looked at her with a pleading expression. "Rillema Construction has an offer on my land, but it's contingent on the purchase of yours."

She gave him a nasty grin, suddenly enjoying herself. "Sorry, I'm not selling."

"Please, Amanda, think about it. Don't say no to spite me. With what you can make off the land, you can buy another farm outright."

At that moment, a police cruiser pulled into the parking lot and slowed to a stop behind her car.

"How are you doing, Amanda?" Frank asked. He nodded at her ex. "Grant."

Grant's face tightened, but his temper held.

"I was talking to Amanda, but I'm leaving." He turned his attention back to her. "Think about it, okay?"

A minute later he was in his car, backing out of his parking space, and gone. Amanda took a breath, relaxed as her heart sought a normal pace.

"You okay?" Frank asked.

"Yes. He was getting very persistent and insisted I listen. Thanks, Frank. How did you know?"

"Nan was watching from the window. She reported a confrontation in the parking lot. I took the call. Knew what the problem might be. Get in your car and I'll follow you home."

"That's not necessary, but thanks. I don't think Grant would dare to follow me to your house."

~ * ~

The call came at three in the morning. "Hello." Amanda listened and woke abruptly. "I'll be there in a few minutes." She threw on jeans and a T-shirt, socks, and athletic shoes and left her room, hoping the call hadn't awakened Frank and Lark. Lark stood in the hallway, looking tired and worried. "Is everything all right?"

"The stable called. Noona's giving birth."

Lark's worried eyes turned bright with excitement. "How wonderful!"

Amanda hesitated. "Do you and the boys want to come along?"

Lark's face lit with pleasure and anticipation. "It won't be a problem?"

"Get them up, but hurry, I promised to be there in a few minutes. I'll go make us a Thermos of coffee."

Lark was already entering the boys' room.

"Me, too?" Frank asked, standing in his bedroom doorway wearing sweatpants and a T-shirt.

"Sure. I'm so nervous, you might have to drive."

He grinned. "I've had practice at this impending motherhood thing." He disappeared back into his room.

By the time the coffee finished brewing, the family had gathered in the kitchen and Lark had poured glasses of orange juice for her two excited but sleepy boys.

Five more minutes and they were in Frank's SUV and on the road. From the back seat, Amanda noticed he stretched the bounds of the speed limit, but there were very few cars on the road.

"I always wonder where people are going at this time of night," Lark said. She looked over her shoulder at her boys in the back, but they were quiet, groggy from sleep, and yawning.

"Some are on their way to work in Traverse City or Grand Rapids," Frank said. "Others, like us, are on special missions."

"Will the baby horse need a cradle?" Rick asked.

"No. Baby horses know how to stand and walk within hours of being born," Amanda said.

"They do? It took Rick a long time to learn to stand," Jack said.

Awake and interested now, the boys asked many questions.

It took ten minutes to reach the barn, and Amanda cursed each mile. *I should be walking out my back door to the barn.*

Lights on a pole glowed over the parking area. Amanda jumped from Frank's SUV and ran to the entrance. Someone had left the double doors cracked open enough for a person to enter. Inside, the smell of horses and their noises filled Amanda's senses with pleasure. She noticed Noona's stall had been draped with canvas to give the mare a sense of privacy and security. The stable was dark except for the glow of light filtering through the cloth around the one stall, but she heard other horses moving and nickering in the darker areas of the barn. Since it was a public stable, the drape would keep other owners from watching the foal and upsetting Noona. Mitch, the stable owner, stood at the stall entrance but came forward to greet her.

"Has it happened yet?" Amanda asked in a low but excitement-threaded voice.

Mitch responded in the same tone. "Not yet, you're in good time. Noona's been circling her stall." He saw Frank, Lark, and the boys enter and nodded at them. "We can raise the canvas on the side of the stall so you can watch. I'll go get crates for the boys to stand on."

"Thanks," Amanda smiled, then turned and squatted in front of Rick and Jack. "You have to be quiet, okay?" The boys nodded.

"We'll make sure," Lark said. "We'll stand right next to them."

Mitch left and returned with two crates and rolled the canvas cover sheltering the stall up far enough for the visitors to watch.

Amanda entered the stall. Uneasy and kicking at her belly, Noona turned and nickered at her. She grasped the mare's halter and rubbed her forehead. Noona pushed her head against Amanda's chest before she swung her head to bite at her own stomach.

Mitch entered, looked at her, and smiled. "You might want to stand back and let her be. She's a little antsy, but settling down to business. I haven't noticed anything to cause alarm."

Amanda moved to the stall door. Noona lay down only to rise back to her feet several times before finally lowering and rolling to her side. Her huge belly and her legs visibly tautened with her effort. Twelve minutes later, Mitch helped pull the foal from Noona. The baby slid from the mare in a whitish sack. Mitch tore the sack at the foal's nose before he stepped back again. Noona rolled from her side onto her folded legs, her sides heaving as she panted from exhaustion. A few minutes later, her head turned toward her foal, and she smelled and nosed her baby, nickering. She began to lick him. In another few minutes, the foal struggled to his feet.

Amanda heard Lark and Frank whispering explanations to Jack and Rick, heard the boys whisper, "Come on, foal, you can do it!"

It was a colt, his wet coat so dark it was hard to tell his color. "Looks like a perfect little colt," Mitch said. "You have a name yet?"

"No, not yet," Amanda answered. Right now, it seemed that naming Noona's colt would only make it that much harder to sell him.

They waited until the foal nursed. Amanda noticed Jack and Rick were yawning. It was time to get them home.

"Thank you for taking care of Noona." She stretched her hand toward Mitch.

"My pleasure. She a fine mare, and her colt is a great looking little fella."

Amanda smiled, but it felt brittle. "Thanks. Come on, Lark, we need to get your boys back to bed."

Lark was already holding Rick, rubbing his back and rocking slightly on her feet. His head lay on her shoulder and he sucked his thumb, already nearly asleep.

"Thank you for letting us tag along," Frank said, picking up Jack, who wrapped his arms around his dad's neck. "None of us has seen a foal born. It's something the boys won't forget."

~ * ~

Amanda was late getting to the office. She hesitated at entering the front door. Edward Van Haitsma waited in the reception area. His gray suit seemed almost out of place in the business casual decor of Brad's office. Wade's business partner rose when she took a few steps into the office.

"Mr. Van Haitsma, this is an unexpected visit."

He smiled. "Ms. Blanchard. I've been waiting to speak with you."

"I'm very late. My horse foaled in the middle of the night."

"So Mrs. Olsen told me. Congratulations."

Over Van Haitsma's shoulder, Amanda saw Nan watching from her desk. Nan's eye-rolling grimace was exactly the expression Amanda would have worn had Van Haitsma not been watching. Instead, she forced a cordial smile and reluctantly invited him back to her office.

Closing the door after Van Haitsma entered, Amanda took off her coat and hung it on a rack in the corner. Settling at her desk, she asked, "What brings you to see me?"

"Amanda, I've come to revisit the offer on your land."

"Wade doesn't want to purchase my land anymore. He said so."

"I know, but since the storm and his accident, he has been under a lot of stress. He's not thinking of the big picture and how your property plays into it."

"So this offer isn't from Wade?"

"No. It isn't from Preston Development. I want to make the purchase."

"Why? To flip it and make a huge profit off it in a year or two?"

"No. Please, let me explain. This project is more mine than Wade's or Rodney's. It was my idea. Rodney, of course, helped draw up the plans under Wade's guidance; but since the inception, this has been my baby. It is very important to me that a competing company doesn't hem us in from future growth. All I'd like you to do is look at the offer and think it over."

"I guess I can do that," Amanda said. "But I'm not going to make a promise one way or another today."

"I understand, but I would like the chance to counter any other offer."

"I doubt that I will sell, Mr. Van Haitsma, but I will look at your offer, and that's all I will promise."

Van Haitsma pulled an envelope from the inside pocket of his suit coat and laid it on her desk as he rose. "That is all I ask. I would hate for this property to become a contentious issue between bidders." He shook her hand and left.

Afterward, Amanda sat at her desk in deep thought. *How did Wade's shooting have anything to do with her land?* Since shortly after her marriage to Grant, she had realized he was a greedy man, and the divorce had proved that, but was he so greedy he'd burn down her house to get her to agree to sell? And would he try to kill Wade to prevent her from selling it to Wade's company? That didn't make sense and wasn't in agreement with what she knew of Grant's normally cowardly personality. Wade had mentioned a problem with the company's books. Was that a reason for Edward Van Haitsma to try and shoot his partner or to burn her house?

She grabbed her purse and coat and told Nan she wouldn't be back today as she rushed through the reception area.

"When your visitor left, I thought you might have more business."

"I promise to make up lost time."

"Don't worry about it, Amanda. You need some personal time now. Work is slow, so go take care of what you need to."

Thirteen

Amanda turned on the cell phone Lark and Frank had given her and tried to dial Wade's number. When she nearly hit an oncoming car, she jerked the wheel right and nearly went off the road. "This thing needs a warning label," she muttered as she pulled off the road and dialed Wade's number. Before he finished saying hello, she asked, "Can you meet me at the First Street Park?"

"Right now? Can't you come to the office?"

"No. Your partner visited my office to make an offer on my property. I don't want him to see me entering your office."

Wade hesitated before saying, "Fifteen minutes."

It took Amanda ten minutes to get to the park. Few cars were parked in the lot as the brisk, late April winds were too cold for the tourist crowds. A wicked offshore breeze blew from off the lake and the crash and rush of breaking waves and retreating water on the sand beach greeted her. Gulls, held aloft on the wind, screeched, their outspread wings hardly moving. White cumulus clouds skittering across the lake toward the land somehow eased her spirit. Sunbeams pushed through the clouds in visible streaks, highlighting Lake Michigan with luminescent green patches amid the otherwise blue-gray waves. Whitecaps streaked across the water. Amanda loved the invigorating wildness of all she sensed. As she walked to the beach, gusts of wind swept her hair back from her head, and abruptly changed direction to whip strands across her face.

She took a deep breath and held her face to the warmth of the spring sun as it emerged from an overhead cloud. "Amanda?" She turned and looked around. Wade approached, his eyes squinting against the wind and cold blowing directly at him. "Are you all right?"

She hardly heard him as her feelings for her surroundings transferred to this man. The full force of her newly recognized love for him rocked her, and she had to hold herself back from the impulse to run to him, to hold him, to seek his kisses as eagerly as she would have as a schoolgirl. She was an adult now, however, and she didn't have time for foolishness. She took refuge in anger, planting her hands on her hips, meeting his gaze.

"When you were at my house during the storm, you mentioned there was something wrong with your books. What was it?"

He stopped short of where she stood, looking down at her from his greater height. His face showed a mixture of relief and conjecture, looking both inquisitive and closed, as if he were afraid to say too much—or expose something undesirable. His gaze shifted out over the lake, while he hunched deeper into his jacket and shoved his hands into its pockets.

"Why do you need to know?"

"Because knowing might give me some answers I need. Tell me, Wade. Please."

He puffed out a long breath, then said, "Three days before your house burned, I downloaded my company's entire hard drive onto a portable drive and drove to Lansing. I know an investigative accountant who agreed to look over the books. He hasn't finished, but he called two nights ago to tell me there are some serious discrepancies."

"Criminal?"

Wade inhaled deeply. "With an accountant of Ed's capability? I doubt he crossed the line into anything illegal, but he certainly maneuvered the accounts. I've since confronted him, and he admitted what he did. You said he made you on an offer on your land?"

"Yes. I've had two. Grant extended one from Rillema Construction, where he will collect a finder's fee, and again this morning, Van Haitsma made an offer."

His face suddenly looked much older. "Do you mind telling me what he said?"

"Basically, he reiterated what he said in your office. My land secured future growth for your proposed project. He seems to think it's his special baby, and is willing to do whatever is necessary to protect it."

"It is. His idea, at least. Most of the accounting shenanigans revolve around the project, too." He finally looked at her. "No matter what he has done to ensure the building of this project, I can't believe he would burn your house down to achieve his goals."

"I don't believe he or Rodney shot at you, either."

Wade exhaled and smiled. "Well, we can agree on that. I've had long talks with Rodney. He was quite shocked at what happened. He isn't a good actor, and he is my brother, so I believe him. Ed, well, he is a partner, but if anything happens to me, only a fraction of the business goes to him. He had no reason to harm me."

"Does he have the resources to make this offer?"

His lips firmed and his gaze traveled toward the water once more. "The last few years, the business has made us both a substantial income. With the right financing, he might well be able to make the offer."

"You knew nothing about this, did you?"

"His offer to you? No. I've already told you I don't want to buy your land."

"So who tried to kill you? You must have given it a lot of thought."

"I have, and I don't think the attack was to kill me, but to frighten me. One that went awry."

"Why do you think so?"

He looked abashed. "Because from the beginning, I've had a good idea who was behind the shooting. I hired a private investigator and he found some circumstantial proof. Enough for me to threaten the person involved. Unfortunately, I never thought they would go after you."

"Melissa?"

He looked across the lake, his lips firming. He finally nodded once.

"And you don't want to hold her accountable?" she asked, her voice rising despite her efforts to remain calm.

"Oh no, I want to hold someone very accountable for what happened to me and, especially to you, but it all starts with proof, and I have nothing substantial." He held out a hand. "Come, let's take a walk while we're here."

"Can you, with your foot?"

"The cast's off. I'm fine."

"And your shoulder?"

"Healing. How are you getting on?"

"All right. Not great. I miss my house. I hate the feeling of being dependent and having to accept charity from my friends. I start at every sound and spook at windblown shadows."

"You'd do the same for them."

"Of course I would. I just don't like being on the receiving end."

"And your horse?"

"Mitch, the owner of the stable, has taken great care of Noona. She foaled."

"That's great. You must be excited about that?"

"No. I'm trying not to get too attached. I mentioned to Mitch I have to sell Noona and her foal." Feeling her eyes begin to water, she looked out over the lakeshore. "He called this morning and said he had someone interested."

"That's good then, isn't it?"

"Good? I don't know. I'll miss Noona dreadfully, but perhaps this is for the best. The sale will tide me over until I receive the insurance, if ever."

"Things will work out, Amanda. You have to believe they will."

Amanda laughed. "Of course they will, just maybe not the way I would like."

"Try being a little more optimistic. Come on, we're on the beach, let's take a walk and let the wind blow our problems away—at least for a little while."

~ * ~

Amanda arrived at Lark and Frank's before her regular time after a normal workday. Although she loved them, she knew it was time to find an interim apartment, and after leaving Wade, she had spent the afternoon apartment hunting. Entering from the garage door, she stopped. Gayle was talking with Lark at the table with drinks and cheese and crackers spread over a platter on the table.

Vic read the newspaper from an upholstered chair near the sliding glass doors.

"Mommy!" Kari yelled and ran to her. Surprised, Amanda held out her arms, grabbed and lifted Kari into a hug. "Oh my goodness! You're here. No one told me you were coming." She glanced up at Gayle. "I didn't see your car."

Smiling, Gayle embraced her in a prolonged hug that included Kari. Amanda wrapped her free arm around her stepmother and whispered, "I'm so sorry about the house. I know you loved it, too." Tears threatened, but she held them back. Gayle didn't, wiping her cheeks as she stepped back.

"I've seen it. We went by there first. Vic was quite surprised to see how much clean-up has been done, and the stone structure that was left."

"It's in amazing condition, Amanda," Vic spoke looking up from the paper, his eyes looking over the rim of his reading glasses.

Carrying Kari, she went to her stepfather and kissed him. "Is that an engineer's or a personal opinion?"

He patted her arm. "A structural engineer's opinion, honey. Only saying, it is possible to rebuild."

"How'd Mom take seeing the house?" Amanda asked in a low voice.

"I can answer for myself," Gayle said. "It was a very sad experience, but I have many wonderful memories." She wiped her cheeks and went on in a cheerier tone, "Vic wanted to let you know, but I said no. You'd only be stressed trying to find us a place to stay. We've already booked into the Ramsdell Inn. We've booked a room for you and Kari, too. She has missed you."

"Did you, sweetheart?" Amanda asked. Kari nodded. "I missed you, too." She hugged Kari.

"Vic's taking us all out to dinner as soon as Frank gets out of the shower," Gayle said.

"They refused to let me make dinner," Lark said, only slightly aggrieved. Amanda knew her friend loved cooking for company but loved going out more.

"After your good care of Amanda, it's the very least we can do," Vic said, folding his paper. He rose and gave Amanda a wink, a hug, and a kiss. "You look good for all the trouble you've been through. We've come to help in whatever way we can."

"Well, dinner will be a very good start," Amanda said. "I'm starving. Where are we going?"

"The casino. We were having drinks and appetizers while we waited for you and Frank. Let Vic fix you something to drink."

Amanda gave an internal sigh of contentment. She picked up a cracker covered with sliced Swiss cheese. "I'd like a seven and seven, thanks, Vic."

"Keep reading, Vic. Let me do that," Lark said, grinning. She picked up a glass before Vic. "I know the mix she likes."

He gave her a mock-gruff look. "I know, too. Weak, with only two ice cubes," Vic smiled his charming best, and Amanda saw Lark had won a new friend. While always friendly, Vic had a flirty smile for the women he liked.

"You knew all about this and said nothing, didn't you?" Amanda guessed, giving Lark a teasing glare.

Lark preened. "Yep."

"Well, I have a surprise, too. I've found a furnished two-bedroom house to rent today. I won't infringe on your hospitality much longer."

"You haven't been infringing on our hospitality," Lark said. "Besides, with you living here, my kids saw a foal born. Do you think that would have happened if you were at the farm? Plus, there's all the help you've given me around the house. I'm going to really miss you. I've enjoyed having you here. Don't feel you have to leave."

"You've made me very welcome, but I have to get my life back on track. Establishing my own, albeit temporary, residence is a start."

Frank entered the kitchen trailing the scent of soap and shaving cream and talk turned to dinner.

"I've booked a table out at the casino," Vic said.

Lark glanced at Amanda. "Do you need to freshen up?" she asked.

"I'd like to change from my work clothes, but I won't be more than a few minutes."

~ * ~

Amanda enjoyed her walleye dinner. The fish entrée was wonderful, and conversation flowed. Gayle shared information about her visit with her sister-in-law, Kari's other grandma, in California. Rick and Jack talked about Noona's baby.

Gayle's face brightened. "How exciting. And you saw it being born?"

Jack nodded. "He tried to stand, but his legs were too bendy."

"Was it a colt or a filly?" Vic asked.

"A beautiful blood bay colt with white stockings on the rear legs. He also has a perfect star on his forehead. He's going to be a beautiful horse," Amanda said.

"What did you name him?" Gayle asked.

"I haven't named him yet."

"Well, congratulations. Looks like you're back in the family business."

Amanda's heart tightened, but she kept smiling. "Perhaps." *And perhaps I'll have to sell both him and Noona to start over.*

"Have you heard from Wade Preston?" Vic asked.

"Yes, I have," Amanda answered. "I've seen him several times. He paid for the site to be cleaned. His parents and brother came to the office and brought me a huge bouquet of roses."

"Have the police discovered anything?" Gayle asked in a sudden lull, looking at Frank.

"Mom, he can't tell us anything," Amanda said. "I'm under investigation on suspicion of arson. Even offering me shelter and being seen here with me could be construed wrongly."

Gayle made a rude sound. "Hardly. You've been friends with Lark for years."

"I'm not on the case," Frank said. "And don't know what is going on with the investigation. My supervisor knows my situation, and to prevent any seeming conflict within the department, I asked to be relieved of any involvement. He agreed."

Gayle gave Frank an apology while she looked at Amanda. "I don't see how they could possibly think Amanda would have set our house on fire."

"Me either," Lark said, patting Gayle's hand.

Gayle talked about her memories of living in the house. "You have to rebuild, Amanda."

Kari was fidgeting. Amanda said, "I need to go to the restroom, how about you, Kari?"

"I'm coming, too," Lark said. "Gayle?"

"No, I'm going to enjoy being alone with the men for a few minutes."

They rose and threaded through the tables. Lark bumped into her at her sudden stop as they reached the entrance.

"Melissa, please, I've done everything you've asked. And you two-time me, with him?"

"Shut-up, Bruce. This is business."

"Business? No! No, it wasn't. You made me promises."

Ahead of her, Amanda saw Melissa Rillema at a table across the wide corridor. The man's raised voice had caught her attention first. A glance showed other people's heads turned toward the commotion. Some stared, some politely went on with whatever engaged them. Amanda had no desire to be polite. There were two men with Melissa, one with his back to her. Melissa tried to calm the man berating her. He was dressed in jeans and a T-shirt with a denim jacket partially hiding the shirt's graphic.

"Keep it down, would you?" said the man with his back to Amanda. "You can't have this discussion now. Not in here."

Amanda started, recognizing that voice. Grant. Quickly, she whispered, "Take Kari to the restroom, would you, Lark?

Glancing at Lark's incredulous expression, she knew her friend had witnessed the same thing she had.

"What are you going to do?" Lark asked her, her voice tense.

"I'm going to see what's going on. It's all right. I will be very discreet, but I want to hear a little more. Go with Lark, Kari," she told her daughter as Lark took the child's hand.

Across the corridor, Melissa rose, her hand briefly touching Grant's. "I'm sorry, Grant, I'll call you later." She walked away.

Amanda was sure Melissa had not noticed her. The man she didn't recognize followed Melissa. Grant threw some money on the table, turned around, and caught Amanda's gaze. He blanched. His expression turned taut. "What are you doing here?" he demanded.

"I'm having dinner with my family. What are you doing? Finalizing your land deal?"

"I'm not going to deny myself an excellent opportunity because of your stubbornness."

"Don't you think you should make sure Melissa isn't being assaulted by that man?"

"Melissa is very good at taking care of herself."

She could barely speak through the surge of anger that whipped her. "As always, you squirm away when confronted with trouble."

"Not at all. We came in different cars, she left of her own accord, and so will I. If she had asked me to escort her, I would have. Goodbye, Amanda." He turned and stalked in the other direction.

Something did not feel right. Amanda quick-stepped, following the direction Melissa had taken. She caught sight of the two in the casino's front foyer. The agitated man was berating Melissa, his hand clasped around her arm.

Catching sight of a security man and realizing he was watching the couple, too, Amanda eased back. Melissa shook off the man's hand and stomped out of the casino. The man followed her, as did the security guard. She hurried along in their wake, but before she reached the front door, she heard rapid footsteps behind her and whirled, ready to do battle if necessary, but it was Frank, not Grant. She went weak with relief, leaning against a wall.

"What's going on?" he asked, breathless. "You're white as a ghost."

Her heart eased its thumping. "I thought you were Grant. I've been witnessing an argument, apparently, but between such interesting acquaintances." Amanda pushed open the door. Outside in the crisp air, she rubbed her bare arms.

"So Lark said."

"Grant was with another couple at a table across from the restaurant's entrance." She moved to partially hide behind the wide stone-based pillars bracing the entrance. It was clear the man with Melissa had not cooled off and actively impeded the woman's desire to escape. He reached for Melissa, but she sidestepped, and he missed. They stood on the sidewalk beyond the drive coming under the portico. Grant jogged down the drive toward the two combatants from the other entrance of the casino further up the driveway.

Amanda watched him approach Melissa. "That snake! He took the other casino exit to hide his movements. So much for being uninvolved."

"That's Bruce Kelder in the jean jacket," Frank said as Grant caught up with Melissa and the other man.

"Leave her alone," Grant yelled, shoving Kelder back from Melissa's path. It only seemed to enrage Bruce. He staggered and fell to one knee, but rose, threatening Grant with his fist.

"Who is he?" Amanda asked Frank, her attention on the threesome.

"She's using you," Bruce shouted. "Like she used me, claiming I was her one and only." The argument turned vile in accusations and epithets.

"The man whose supposedly stolen truck was the vehicle whose driver or passenger we believe shot Wade and forced him off the road," Frank spoke low, but his voice covered up some of the argument. The confrontation had attracted a few more of the casino's security men.

Two guards joined the first one and asked the trio to leave, but Melissa nodded at Bruce. "He's too drunk to drive."

One of the guards asked, "Have you been drinking, sir?" Bruce ignored the man. He yelled at Melissa. "You bitch! After all I've done for you! Do you think I'm going to let you dump me now? Or do you believe I'll take whatever blame you want to evade? I'm not taking the rap for burning that house down. I did it on your orders."

Amanda's heart stopped before lurching into hard beating motions. She released a pent-up breath.

"Interesting," Frank said, pulling his cell phone from a pocket.

"Shut up, Bruce. You're so drunk you don't know what you're saying." Melissa turned to one of the guards. "We broke up recently, and he's been making ridiculous accusations against me ever since."

Two guards grabbed Bruce's arms and pulled him away from Melissa. He struggled with the men holding him, shouting, "I won't go down for you, bitch." Over the guard's shouted warning, Amanda couldn't hear what else Bruce said to the guards.

Amanda felt a prick of pleasure at seeing the woman's frightened reaction. Grant wrapped his arms around Melissa, and Amanda's lip curled. She knew what she'd heard and seen. This wasn't just a business meeting. *What gall! What a liar. What a deserving couple!*

One of the guards said something to Melissa and Grant that Amanda couldn't hear.

Melissa's overly loud voice carried clearly. "I'm not going anywhere but home. I've done nothing wrong except being attacked by a raving drunk who has been stalking me. I don't know what house he is referring to. How could I?"

After another unheard comment from the guard, she said, "No, I don't have a restraining order. This stalking behavior only began recently when I started dating again. I didn't want to ruin his life, and I've not been in fear of my life until this moment."

Amanda heard Frank speaking on his cell phone but was so engrossed in eavesdropping she didn't pay much attention to what he said. She knew he had called the sheriff's department.

A casino SUV with lights flashing pulled up and security forced Bruce into it. One guard continued to talk with Melissa and Grant for a few minutes before the two walked away into the parking lot.

Frank put away his cell phone. "Why don't you go back to our table? I'd like to have a few words with security." He left her side as the guards came into the porch area.

Curious, but trusting Frank, Amanda did as he asked. She heard one guard say the word intoxicated before the door closed behind her. When she took her seat at the table, everyone looked at her expectantly. "Frank will rejoin us shortly. He's speaking with casino security."

"Did he call the department?" Lark asked.

"Yes, he did. It seems Melissa's old boyfriend is stalking her, and Grant, who said he was only here on business, appears to be her new boyfriend. He actually tried to protect her. Unfortunately, her ex-boyfriend made a few accusations Frank wanted to report."

"Does he think this man is behind all your problems?" Vic asked.

She shrugged. "I don't know, but I thought it an interesting relationship. He mentioned something about torching a house on her orders, which she, of course, denied."

"That rat deserves whatever happens to him," Gayle said.

"Bruce?" Amanda asked.

"No, Grant! Who's Bruce?"

"The man the casino detained."

"Him, too."

Amanda smiled at Gayle's comment about her ex. She'd said what Amanda felt. Exhaling an exhausted breath, she pushed a strand of Kari's hair into place. "I agree. I think he has finally found the woman he deserves."

"Everyone finished?" Vic asked, "Let's go."

Frank joined them as they reached the foyer. He looked serious, but he smiled at her as they approached. He thanked Vic for the dinner and the two launched into what seemed to be a conversation on golf before they reached the car. To Amanda, it seemed like Frank was trying to avoid her gaze.

"Frank?" He looked at her. "I know the position this has put you in. I'm glad you were there to see that, but your family and your job come first. There is no conflict in that."

"Thanks, Amanda. Luckily, tonight there were other witnesses."

Fourteen

Amanda slept next to Kari that night, though the hotel room held another bed. She needed to have her little girl with her. Though trouble loomed, at least Kari was safe. She listened to Kari breathing, her mind too busy to sleep.

Grant and that horrible encounter at the restaurant filled her thoughts. *How could I have fallen for Grant's smooth talk and manipulations when he was courting me? Why hadn't I seen his inherent dishonesty earlier, before I married him? Had I loved him? I must have, or had I been in love with being in love? Had he loved me?* She doubted that now, but did he hate her? *Had he been in on the plot to burn my house, even if he hadn't actually lit the torch himself?*

"Can my judgment have been that bad?" she whispered quietly so as not to wake Kari. She edged to one side, trying to find a position comfortable enough to invite sleep.

Her efforts failed as Wade's image rose in her mind to supplant that of Grant. Buck had found him in her orchard. *Was that some sort of strange coincidence, or was it karma? Good karma or bad?* She envisioned him naked on her kitchen floor as he was after she had undressed him. His kiss. Her body twitched with lust at that memory, of the more recent one, the kisses in the elevator.

Groaning, she rolled onto her back and put a pillow over her face. She pulled it off to look at Kari. Wade was certainly a strong, self-assured man. Unlike Grant, he had no problem relating to Kari, easily playing, reading, and laughing with her while they were snowbound. He seemed to enjoy Kari's company.

But the thought came at her...after Grant, how could she trust her judgment about any man? Is Wade another user? *Am I deluding myself that he has some interest other than gratitude? What do I know about him?* Wade was a self-made man, well-educated, head of a successful business. He was a great kisser. So what? He didn't need to marry someone for financial gain. She laughed at considering herself a bride bringing financial gain. Bride? Oh Lord. Where did that idea come from?

But how was Grant tied to Melissa? Has she bought my land... Grant's land? And is Wade, despite his protestations of innocence, all a part of it?

If so, who had tried to kill him, and what did it have to do with me?

She sighed as her thoughts ran full circle, desperately wanting to sleep, and knowing it wasn't going to happen.

~ * ~

The phone rang, starling Amanda from sleep she didn't remember falling into. She felt disoriented and fumbled with the phone receiver. "Amanda?"

"Oh, hi Mom."

Kari stirred next to her, opened her eyes, and smiled. She didn't make any move to get out of bed.

"Were you asleep?" Gayle asked. "I didn't mean to wake you."

Amanda looked at the clock. Lord, it was eight-thirty. "That's okay. What's up?"

"I want to see your rental house. Vic and I want to help you get it ready. Hurry up and come downstairs. Vic is hungry and wants to buy breakfast."

She groaned. "Kari and I will meet you in half an hour. Is that okay?"

"Yes. Vic can take a walk and we'll have coffee until you join us."

"Order a pot and an extra cup."

"Done."

Hanging up the phone, Amanda smiled at Kari. "Good morning. We've slept in. Grandma wants us downstairs quick. I have to take a shower. Can you dress while I'm in the bathroom?"

"Can I watch TV?"

"Yes. I'm sure there are some cartoons on. Would you like that?"

"Yes."

"Okay, then, let's get a move on."

The phone rang.

"Morning, Ms. Blanchard. This is Mitch Henkins from the North View Stable. Calling to tell you I sold Noona and her foal yesterday. I have a check for you anytime you come by."

Her heart squeezed. *Sold.* She bit her lip and squeezed her eyes tight to prevent any emotion from escaping as she thanked him. "I'll be by this afternoon."

~ * ~

Amanda sipped coffee as she listened to Gayle over the dishes holding their breakfast remains. "You don't have much to pack, so Vic and I'll help you move tomorrow. You'll want to have Kari with you. Although you could stay with Vic and me if you wanted."

"Staying in Onekama would make the commute to work too far. I'd rather be closer. Plus, Kari will be with her usual daycare provider. She knows the children there, and I think it will make her more comfortable."

The waitress came by and picked up the dishes, offering to refill coffee cups. Amanda gratefully accepted.

"You'll probably need help today to get the house clean."

"The house was clean when I looked at it, but I'd like to put fresh paint on the walls. The owner gave me permission, but at my own cost. I want white on the walls. Right now, the kitchen is the color of overcooked peas, with both bedrooms bright pink and the living room is off-white, but dirty looking."

"Well, we'll clean anyway, so it's our clean."

Amanda nearly choked at Gayle's often-repeated comment. Gayle never thought anyone cleaned to her expectations.

"Amanda, finish that coffee so we can go. Or would you like to take a cup to go?" Vic asked.

"I would be grateful," she said, smiling at him.

He nodded, picked up the bill and went to the register. Gayle fussed with Kari, wiping her granddaughter's mouth, brushing crumbs off her pink lace-trimmed T-shirt. "Did you get enough to eat? Do you want to go to the bathroom?" Gayle asked as Kari climbed off her chair. Looking at the yellow sweatpants and the purple pony embroidered on the T-shirt, she asked, "Did you pick out your clothes this morning?"

"Yes," Kari smiled proudly. "They're my favorites." Gayle frowned at Amanda.

"The pink trim on the pants nearly matches the shirt," Amanda said, pulling Kari's jacket into place. "Look, Vic's finished paying...let's go." She kissed Vic as he handed her a large container of coffee. "My mom was very lucky to find you."

"I think so, too," he said, grinning.

They stopped at Lark's house so Amanda could pick up her belongings. Rick and Jack took Kari to the back yard to play with Buck. Frank put a hand on Amanda's arm as they passed in the hallway, detaining her.

"There is nothing I can tell you because I know nothing. Yesterday, I alerted the proper authorities to what looked like a suspicious association."

Amanda nodded, while her throat tightened. "I know." Since seeing Grant with Melissa, her imagination had worked overtime. No matter how two such unlikely people had come together, it only meant one more betrayal by Grant. How could she have been so blind? He was greedy, yes, opportunistic, yes, but evil? It was hard to endure the fact that she had been married to him. That he had touched her intimately and, even if divorced, felt so little that he could treat her so callously.

"Frank, why don't you supervise the boys getting ready, find the paint stuff and collect your toolbox?" Lark shouted from the kitchen. Frank glanced at Amanda with a grin. "Drill sergeant at work. We'll see you there." He headed for the basement.

A minute later, Lark found her. "We'll follow you as soon as we're done here. I have to pick up the kitchen, and I found a few things around the house that were duplicates, so I'm giving them to you. There are a couple bags in the kitchen."

"I'll get them," Vic said. Lark handed Gayle a bag of sheets and towels. "They're not much, so don't thank me, but they'll work until you can get some new ones."

"I'll go put these in the car," Gayle said.

"You've done so much for me," Amanda said, hugging Lark. "Thank you. I'll never be able to repay you."

"Nonsense, none of us knows what the future holds, but I know you'll always be there for me, too." Her face became serious. "I know you probably won't say anything, but I think Grant has finally shown his true colors. What a rat."

"You're denigrating rats," Amanda said.

Lark smiled. "You haven't said much about your encounter with him."

Amanda shrugged. "I did have an encounter with Grant, but now he knows I know what a colossal jerk he is." She waited for one breath, "Then I realized what a fool I'd been to ever fall for his flattery and declarations of devotion. It's all very humiliating.

"But you're free of him. It cost you a lot, but you have Kari, and your mom and Vic, and your friends. Your land. It has a considerable value even without the house."

"That's true. It holds so many memories of when my father was alive, and when my grandparents lived there. Plus, I'll never have the barn and riding arena anywhere else." She'd known for a long time she could rebuild her life for the better without Grant dragging her down, and now she knew where she would rebuild the life she needed. Right there, where her heart's home was, Stone House Farm—though she might have to do without the stone house for some time.

She hugged Lark. "There is no doubt I came out way ahead when we became friends."

"Are you going to be all right?"

"Yes, I am. I'm not going to think about how foolish I was."

"Anyone can be fooled by a good manipulator, Amanda. The only pity is never waking up to the fact you've been used."

Laughing, Amanda said, "With that, I'm leaving." She went to the kitchen and called to Kari.

"Can we take Rick and Jack with us? Can Buck come?"

"Not today. Jack and Rick have agreed to take care of him for a few more days. He'll come once we settle into the house."

"Leave Kari here with the boys," Lark said. "My mom is babysitting, and Kari will get bored cleaning and painting a rental house."

"You're sure?" Amanda asked dubiously. "Won't your mom mind?"

"I told her to expect Kari, and she didn't mind at all."

"Would you like that?" Amanda asked Kari.

"Yes," Kari said, looking happier.

"Okay, then. You stay and play with Jack, Rick, and Buck. You behave yourself."

Once Vic backed out of the drive, Amanda's mind mulled over many conflicting thoughts. *Was Wade another user?* She didn't want to believe it, but how would she ever know if his interest was engaged? *How could I ever trust anyone again? That was stupid. Her family loved her. Frank and Lark, Brad and Nan Olson had been constantly supportive and encouraging. Friends she knew were completely reliable. I have to be careful who I choose to trust.*

After Gayle was satisfied the rental house was really clean, Vic drove them to the stables so Amanda could pick up the check for Noona.

"I'm sorry you had to sell her, honey," Gayle said. "It must feel like losing your dad all over again."

"Yes, it does, but at least she'll help Kari and me start fresh."

Inside Noona's stall, she rubbed her mare's head. Part of her was sad Kari couldn't say goodbye to Noona. Another part was glad. Kari would never understand leaving the foal.

It broke her heart, but she pasted a smile on her face as she wiped away the tears. Gayle hugged her, patting her back in comfort. "It'll be all right, sweetie. Good things are yet to come. You sometimes have to wait out the not so good."

After leaving the stable and depositing the counter check with a name Amanda didn't recognize at her bank, they went shopping for a few pieces of furniture and necessities at her new home. When they reached the house, Gayle sniffed at the somewhat run-down exterior but declared a little paint would make the interior quaint.

"Let's get the living room painted before the furniture van arrives," Vic said, bringing paint cans into the house.

Lark, Frank, Nan, and Brad Olson arrived a few hours later to help paint. Vic checked out the furnace, electrical, and plumbing. He changed washers in the faucets and rewired two outlets he deemed faulty. Gayle lined the kitchen drawers and shelves with paper. A little while later, she disappeared with Lark while Amanda and Nan painted Kari's room. Lark returned with each arm clutching bags of groceries followed by Gayle and Wade Preston carrying more bags.

Wade wore old jeans and a ratty-looking sweatshirt, neither of which diminished his good looks. His smile made Amanda want to disregard her resolve to remain uninvolved until she was sure he was trustworthy. *Go slow. Be sure.*

Surprise kept her quiet until Gayle nudged her in the back with her elbow. "Hello, Wade, I didn't expect to see you."

His smile singed the edges of her resolve, and her attitude felt like a lit candle—slowly melting.

"I heard you had a new place and came over with a housewarming gift. I'll be right back." Wade put his grocery bags on the worn kitchen counter, turned, and left. He returned a few minutes later. Frank helped him carry a large box, the outside printed with features and details of the television inside. They quickly went into the living room and put the box down.

"Good idea," her mother said. "Amanda doesn't have one. You left so quickly Amanda couldn't introduce me." She held out her hand. "Hi, I'm Gayle Estees, Amanda's stepmom. I've heard a lot about you."

"Not all bad, I hope," Wade said, taking her hand. "Where are Buck and Kari?"

"They're at Lark's while we're cleaning and painting," Gayle said. "Dogs, kids, and paint are a bad mix."

His gaze caught Amanda's. "You're no longer worried about any danger?" he asked.

"I think any threat ended with what Frank and I witnessed at the casino."

Wade nodded. "I heard. You're probably right."

Amanda wondered who had told him. "What did you hear?" she asked.

"The sheriff called me on the way here, told me Bruce Kelder is being held on charges of assault with a deadly weapon and arson."

"He shot you?" Amanda whispered. "But...why?"

Before Wade could answer, Lark entered the living room, talking on her cell phone and holding an overflowing box. She clicked the phone shut. "I've put the groceries away and Nan brought some of her extra kitchen utensils. The box is in the kitchen." Lark grinned at Amanda, then stood right in front of her so only Amanda saw her joyous, surprise-filled face and raised eyebrows.

She mouthed, "He came with gifts, too!"

"That's good news," Gayle said, answering Wade. "Not that you're getting shot was good, but that they finally have the culprit."

"Wow!" Lark said, stepping away. "They do? They have the perp? Was it Kelder? Did he say why he did it?"

"He wanted Melissa back," Wade said with a shrug, "and thought if he got rid of me, she'd return to him."

That struck Amanda as odd, but both Frank and Wade were pulling the staples on the box as Wade added, "It was a relief to learn who was behind it." Once the men had the box open, Frank helped Wade take the set out of the packaging.

"Kelder confessed and has been arrested on arson and assault with a deadly weapon," Frank said, folding cardboard into small pieces. "But he claims another person is involved. That person hasn't been questioned, but will be. I just heard myself. The sheriff called a few minutes ago, while I was out in the yard."

"I'm glad to hear it," Vic said, listening from the hallway. Brad and Nan stood behind him, drawn by all the voices. "Did he have anything to do with Amanda's car?"

"He set the fire, but that's all I know," Frank said, looking at Amanda. "He might have punctured the brake line as well but hasn't been questioned on that yet. But if he did, at least he's in custody, so you're safe from him."

Relief rushed through her so fast she nearly lost her breath. Through her tears, she saw Vic hug Gayle. Seeing an echo of her relief on Gayle's face, Amanda realized how worried her mom had been. She cleared her throat and exhaled. "That's very good news!"

"News worth celebrating," Vic said as Lark hugged Amanda. "I brought some champagne to celebrate a new house, but now we have more to celebrate."

He walked into the kitchen, followed by Gayle who was saying, "I put the glasses in the cupboard. Not champagne flutes, but..."

"No buts," Vic said. "I brought flutes, too."

Lark laughed. "Anyhow, between my dishes and Nan's pans, you have enough to get you started until you can get some replacements. Good Lord. They delivered the sofa while I was gone. I love it." She hugged Amanda, "and I'm so glad this is over."

"Do you have a trash bag?" Frank asked, the broken-down cardboard box under his arm. He gave the living room's interior an appraising look. "Looks like you did a good job out here."

"I have a little more to do in the bathroom," Amanda said.

"I can help paint," Wade said.

Frank grinned. "All help is gratefully accepted. We have this room to finish and the kitchen. Glad to see you under better circumstances, Preston."

"Brad and I will do the other bedroom as soon as we finish the one we're in," Nan said.

Frank's cell phone rang, and he walked away, speaking for a few minutes. From his words, Amanda knew it was a work-related call.

After a minute, he said, "Wait, I'll ask her." He turned to her. "Tom Stiles, the officer who talked with you at our house is on the line. He wants to speak with you." He handed her his phone.

"This is Amanda Blanchard."

"Ms. Blanchard, I wanted to tell you that you have been cleared of any suspicions involving your house fire. We have a suspect in custody, and he has indicated there is a coconspirator."

"Grant Carter?"

"I won't name the people under suspicion until we have proof of their complicity. We do know Kelder tampered with the brake lines on your car. I doubt anyone will consider causing you any trouble knowing Kelder is in custody, but you might want to be careful. The co-conspirators he named will be brought in for questioning, but we need more to hold them on than what we have. I've told Frank the details. I'm leaving it to him to answer your questions."

"Thank you. It's a relief to know I'm cleared of arson and insurance fraud."

When she handed the phone back to Frank, Gayle was passing champagne flutes. "Well, now you'll have the insurance money. You can start to make plans. Maybe you'd like to sell the land and start over somewhere else?"

She didn't want Gayle to start worrying, so decided not to mention what else the sheriff had said. "I'm not sure of anything yet." Frank gave her a look that told her he knew about Tom's warning, but he wouldn't tell anyone.

"You have a lease here, or month by month?" Wade asked.

"Monthly."

Gayle smiled. "Then you will be able to get out of it quickly, if needed. With the insurance money, you could be in a new home within months."

"Yes, I could."

Frank grimaced. "Great. Let's get to work and get the place painted, then." He heaved a dramatic sigh. "Before I have to help paint some new place."

Amanda laughed. "I'll probably be here long enough to make your efforts worthwhile, Frank."

Late that afternoon, the house smelled of paint but was clean and livable. Amanda thanked everyone as she watched them leave. Wade had been called away an hour before on a construction site problem.

"You will spend the night with us. You and Kari don't want to sleep in that smell," Lark said.

"Thanks, but Gayle and Vic have the hotel rooms for a week, so I've a place to stay." Gayle and Vic had left earlier to pick up Kari. Vic had brought over her car, so only she, Frank, and Lark were left by the back door. "I'll lock up here and be on my way." She hugged Lark. "Thank you, thank you for everything." Her voice grew husky, and her vision blurred as she held her friend.

"What are friends are for? My pleasure."

"Do you want me to help you lock up?" Frank asked.

"No. I don't think anyone will renew any grudge they felt against me right now. Why would they when they're already under suspicion? Plus, in a few minutes, I'll be at the hotel with Gayle and Vic."

"Woman's logic." Frank shook his head. "We'll wait while you close up the house and follow you in the car."

"That's not necessary. Lark is exhausted—take her home. I'll be leaving in minutes."

Frank looked uncertain. "No, really, go," Amanda insisted.

Amanda waved as the car pulled out of the drive. After a moment of watching the car leave, she went into the house to close and lock the bedroom windows. Finished, she came out of what would be Kari's room but was startled as she nearly bumped into Grant. He leaned negligently against the doorframe, a smile curving his lips, but not reaching his eyes.

Gasping, Amanda pressed her hand to her chest. "Why are you here? What do you want?"

Grant's smile never wavered. "I had to see you. Your phone is disconnected. I knew you had been staying with Lark, so I followed her here, and I waited for everyone to leave. The front door was open, so I came in."

"Well, you can leave the same way."

"Wait." He put out a hand to detain her as she moved. "No matter what has happened between us, you have to know I would never set fire to the house."

She jerked free. "Let go of me," she said, standing her ground. "What makes you think I'd believe anything you say?"

"Come on, Amanda." He waved his other arm in a dismissive, you're-smarter-than-this motion, but continued to fill the doorway with his body, trapping her inside. "You're mad because I demanded my fair share in the property settlement, but don't punish me with arson charges to get even." He rubbed his mouth with his hand.

"I didn't bring any charges. I've left that to the police."

"I wouldn't harm you or Kari. You know I wouldn't."

"Do I? You tried to get me to sell my land in a scheme that would make you money from my loss."

He shrugged. "That's business. I needed money and the divorce judge was unfair in the distribution of assets. I deserved more. That doesn't mean I burnt your house down." He raised his hand. "That was all Melissa—she's a user, and I caught on too late. She wanted Preston to pay for dumping her. Your property became a means to achieve her revenge when he refused to take her back. If she got your land, it would wreck his company's plans and pay you back for taking him from her."

"Me? Take him from her? That's insane. There's nothing between me and Wade, and even if there were, burning my house is a bit excessive, don't you think? Kari could have been injured or killed, let alone me!"

Grant shrugged. "She knew you'd sent Kari away with Gayle."

"You knew all this, and did nothing?" Amanda backed away, out of range, wishing the empty room held some kind of a weapon, a paint can, anything, but it had all been cleaned up. "You deserved nothing from our divorce! It's my family's property, my heritage. You brought nothing to the marriage, left with all our savings, and the judge decided in your favor." In her fury, she lunged toward him. "Get out of my way and get out of my house."

He took a deep breath, and slumped, looking vulnerable. Amanda had seen this act before. His face changed, softened into hurt bewilderment. "Rehashing the past is getting us nowhere. You'll get an insurance settlement that will let you buy another house. I'm sorry it happened, but please, you have to believe me. I truly didn't know about her plans to hurt Preston or to burn your house. Call the police and tell them the truth. Do it for me, Mandy, for old time's sake. I'm innocent. You can vouch for me."

"I won't lie for you, and I can't believe you came here to ask me to give you a character reference. Do I believe you could set fire to my house? No. But my judgment about you was quite wrong from the beginning, so I'm not telling the police anything about you. And you should be very happy about that."

His demeanor changed from pleading to furious. "Damn it, Amanda. It's only a call."

"I think the police will want information, like proof of your whereabouts on the times in question. You should be thinking about that, not about getting me to vouch for you. So what if I did as you asked and called? It means nothing to the police."

"It does if they only have a confessed criminal's word against mine."

"I thought you'd run to her." The voice startled Amanda. Melissa stood in the bedroom's doorway. Her face lacked emotion except for her scowling lips, but she wore no makeup and her eyes were rimmed with red. She looked as if she hadn't slept in a year. Her body looked shapeless in worn jeans and an oversized sweatshirt. Her hair was stuffed into a baseball cap. She held a small handgun. Every thought Amanda held crystallized into one. *She's deranged!*

"Melissa?" Grant twirled away from Amanda to face the woman, fear edging his voice and face. "What are you doing here?"

"I followed you here and listened to your pathetic pleading, you snake. You say you love me, but you run to her. Do you think she is going to save you? I'm going to make you pay for betraying me, like I did Wade." She glanced at Amanda. "And you for ruining my life."

"That's not true," Amanda said. "I haven't done—"

Melissa's aimed the gun in her direction. "Shut up! You stole Wade."

"Only after you shot him." The accusation popped out without her thinking, but if she were to die, she wanted the truth.

Melissa took a step into the room, keeping the gun aimed at her, her hand shaking, but her eyes wild. "He had to pay. So did you." Tears seemed odd on the emotionally flat expression.

"And my daughter, too?"

"She wasn't home." The gun shook harder.

"What about the brakes on my car? She was in the car."

"I had nothing to do with that."

"No," Amanda agreed, "You had Bruce do it for you."

"Bruce has always loved me, would do anything to make me happy. But he spent time in prison, so could never marry me, even if he were rich, which he isn't. I didn't know what he planned to do. The little girl shouldn't have been in the car. Bruce was only supposed to scare you like he was only supposed to scare Wade." Melissa wiped her cheeks with her free hand. "He promised to help me. Like he did." She pointed the gun at Grant. "He was going to get you to sell your property. I wanted to steal Wade's plans, control the land he wanted. That would have shown him he couldn't discard me! Wade would have crawled to me on my terms."

"Now they've all betrayed you," Amanda said.

"Yes, exactly." Melissa aimed a rage-filled gaze at Grant. "Now that you don't think you're going to get any money, you want to blame me."

"He's good at that. He always blames someone else for his failures."

"Amanda, for God's sake shut up," Grant said, backing up against the wall. "Can't you see she's unhinged?"

Melissa squealed. "I am not crazy! You're trying to save your skin."

"That's because I had nothing to do with any criminal activity."

Melissa smiled. "When they find you here, in her house, it will be deemed a murder-suicide, and all the blame will fall on you."

"Amanda, are you all right?" Wade shouted from somewhere, probably the kitchen. Amanda froze. *No. No!* Melissa turned to the door, her gun hand waving between her and Grant.

Amanda heard his footsteps in the living room. "I saw your car was outside, and Frank and Lark are gone. I left my watch on the kitchen counter. Amanda?"

Grant cowered against the wall. She saw the anger in Melissa's gaze, the determination as the other woman's attention centered on the footsteps coming down the hall.

Leaping forward, she grabbed Melissa's gun arm and shoved it upward. "Wade! Get out! Gun!"

Melissa turned her gaze back on Amanda, her look hate-crazed, her voice also raised in a scream. In a quick motion, Amanda moved one hand to grasp the hand holding Melissa's gun, then the other until both her hands held the gun Melissa clutched. The woman was incredibly strong, and Amanda struggled for her life.

The gun went off with shocking loudness. Wade appeared. In one flying movement, he tackled Melissa, taking her to the floor. Amanda, with a death grip on her hands, fell with her. The gun went off a second time. Wade scrambled with Melissa, but his greater strength prevailed. Seconds or minutes might have passed. Amanda was too stunned to be sure.

Wade held Melissa in a wrestler's hold, one she couldn't escape. "Are you okay?"

When she didn't immediately respond, he asked, louder. "Amanda, are you okay?"

Sense returned. "Yes." She looked around the room in wonder. "Yes. Both bullets hit the walls." She pointed at the holes, hearing Wade heave a breath of relief.

Grant rose and ran for the door, but stopped as Frank entered with a drawn gun. He assessed the situation. "Stay," he told Grant while he quickly handcuffed Melissa, who broke down weeping hysterically. Pulling his cell phone from his pocket, Frank called the sheriff's office.

Everything happened so fast, Amanda barely had time to catch her breath. She crawled a few feet from Melissa and sat on the floor, watching as Wade rose, staring down at Melissa. After a long moment, he looked at her.

"What are you doing here?" Wade demanded. Grant started when Wade spoke to him and took a backward step out of the room, but Frank ordered him to stop. He turned pale. Before Grant could answer, Wade turned to Amanda. "Did he harm you?"

"No," Amanda said once, then raised her voice and said no in an audible voice.

Grant stepped away from the door. "I was here to talk to Amanda. Melissa followed me here."

Frank looked at her. She nodded in confirmation. *How did he get here so fast?*

As if reading her mind, Frank said, "As we rounded the block, Lark saw someone lurking on the sidewalk. I turned around halfway down the block and came back."

"Did you want to talk to him?" Wade asked her, nodding his head at Grant.

"No, I didn't."

Frank took over. "Wade, take Amanda to the living room. Watch for the sheriff." They could hear sirens in the distance. "You," he ordered Grant, "wait here where I can watch you."

"Fine. I'm not guilty of anything. Amanda heard, and she can vouch for me."

Amanda looked at Grant. "I've said all I'm going to say. If you want help, get a lawyer."

Grant's jaw jutted angrily, but Wade helped her rise and placed an arm around her shoulders as her legs seemed too shaky to stand. He pulled her from the room. Within minutes, there was a knock at the door and two sheriff's deputies entered. Shortly, Frank and the other deputies escorted both Grant and Melissa from the house. Relieved, she heard the front door close.

Lark entered from the kitchen. "Oh my God! Are you okay? What happened? Where's Frank? When he heard that shot, he charged in here..." Lark threw her hand over her mouth to stop sobbing. It didn't work.

"He's okay," Wade explained because words had failed Amanda. Another deputy entered the house with Frank behind him. "I thought I told you to stay in the car?" he yelled at Lark.

"I waited until I saw the sheriff's car arrive. I had to know what was going on."

Frank calmed down, pulled Lark into a hug. "One of the deputies will need to take your statement, Amanda. Come on," he said, pulling Lark into the kitchen. She heard him talking but didn't listen.

"You were crazy brave," Wade said, his arm tightening around her.

"She was going to shoot you. I didn't know what else to do. Did you find your watch?" Her question sounded inane to her own ears.

He held up the timepiece to her. "Yes. I also came because I wanted to ask you to dinner. Thought I'd check to see if you were still here before going to Frank and Lark's. I figured after all your hard work you might be hungry. Are you truly okay?" His tone spoke of his doubts. "You shouldn't have let him in. He isn't cleared of anything yet." Wade's face was intent with concern.

"I didn't. He came in while I was locking the windows. He demanded I tell the police he is innocent, and while I want to believe he wouldn't harm me, I'll leave it to the police to prove. One way or another." She felt her jaw tighten. "However, then Melissa showed up. I don't believe they had proof against either Grant or Melissa, other than a confession that might have been motivated by vengeance at seeing her with another man. So why did she come here? She must be crazy."

"Kelder claims Melissa was in the truck with him, driving as he fired at me. It makes sense. He couldn't have driven and shot, too. He claims he never meant to hit me, only scare me."

"Why? Why would she do that?"

"Anger. Melissa has a history of doing whatever it takes to get her way. I realized that a long time ago, which is why I broke off our engagement, but I didn't know the lengths she would go to. Who would think anyone would be so, so—"

"Obsessive?"

"Single-minded. She never loved me except for my money and what she believed my social standing to be, plus I was in the same business as her father. After you left the office that day, I told her to get lost. She said she'd get even and made an even more dramatic exit than you did. She knew of Ed and Rodney's project plans."

He looked embarrassed. "After our initial break up, I knew she had talked her dad into a plan to counter our development near your property, but I didn't worry about it. I thought it a petty gesture. We had the property we needed, or so I thought. I didn't know how far she would take things. That's what I wanted to tell you tonight. It was my fault your house was burned. Can you forgive me?"

She stared at him. He was serious. "You didn't do anything. Melissa was behind everything that happened to me...and you. She must be crazy." Tension drained out of her in one heartbeat. Her stomach grumbled and she laughed a little wildly. "You have nothing to be forgiven for, but you did mention dinner...maybe after everything here is over? Somewhere quiet?"

~ * ~

As Amanda entered the office the next day, Nan jumped up. "Have you heard?"

"Heard what?"

"Bruce Kelder has been arrested for shooting Wade, and Melissa Rillema is implicated in a conspiracy to do bodily harm. It was on the news this morning."

"Any mention of Grant?"

"No, but there is mention of a land deal to ruin her former fiancé's plans. There is a witness who has come forward."

"Grant. He came to see me last night. Wanted me to tell the sheriff he didn't set fire to my house."

Nan swore. "Always the user."

Amanda laughed. "He took my advice. I told him if he wanted help to get a lawyer. But that was after Melissa showed up."

Nan gasped.

Amanda told her about the previous evening's visit.

Nan hugged her. "That wasn't on the news. You were so brave. Oh, dear, you could have been hurt, but you stood up to both of them. Good for you."

~ * ~

Amanda walked the beach, occasionally skipping stones. The last week of April had brought sun, unexpected warmth, and a sense of normality. Kari ran ahead gathering shells and rocks, and Buck ran circles around Kari or chased gulls before running back to Amanda. It felt good to see Kari so happy. Watching her play brought memories of her childhood and playing with Marla. A tinge of sadness that her cousin was gone mixed with her nostalgia. She and Kari could move on now. "She's a great little girl, Marla. You would be proud."

Picking up another smooth stone off the hard-packed sand, Amanda skillfully pitched it and watched her missile skip four times on the water's surface. A wave broke over her athletic shoes. The water was freezing. She ran back onto the loose dry sand behind her.

She took a deep breath and raised her face to the sun, enjoying its warmth. Finally, the mess that had started at the beginning of the month was over. The question was what to do now? Noona and her colt were gone, bought practically the moment she contacted Mitch Henkins. There would be no more horses. The insurance check might be enough to build another house, but not rebuild the house that had been.

She and Kari walked through the pasture and took the path between the two orchards. The apple trees were in full bloom. She turned and looked behind her. The land dropped to show Lake Michigan glinting in shades of blue and green in the bright sunlight. Amanda briefly remembered it covered in ice and snow, as it had been only a few months earlier.

The sound of a truck engine drew her attention. She walked toward the house, but only the bare walls stood amid the burned-bare tree branches, almost how she imagined the broken ramparts of some ancient castle would appear. Kari ran ahead with Buck, who raced and barked madly as he passed Kari. When Amanda finally reached the house, she saw a black truck with a horse carrier hitched to it in the driveway. Wade Preston held and hugged Kari. Kari hugged him back. Buck bounced around them, barking.

Amanda heard Kari giggle and chatter while her own breath caught in her throat. Wade put Kari down as she approached. Mitch

Henkins was leading Noona and her foal into the paddock. Ferd stood with them. She bit her lip as she approached Wade. His mouth spread into a more engaging smile.

"I brought you another gift. I called Tina. She said she would come by to take care of the horses, even sleep in the barn if she had to. She's happy to have Ferd closer to her home."

"Can I pet the baby, Mommy?" Kari asked, taking her hand and tugging her toward the paddock. Wade unlatched the gate and they entered the enclosed area. Noona ambled up to them. Amanda caught Noona's halter.

"Be careful. Colts can be skittish." Mitch grabbed the colt's halter and held it while Kari ran a hand down the colt's neck.

"Yeah. He found out the hard way," Mitch said, nodding at Wade.

Wade rubbed his thigh. "Yes, I did."

The colt's oversize equine eye watched Kari's movement, but the little horse remained calm. Amanda rubbed Noona's forehead.

Mitch smiled. "Hold this colt, Wade. I got to get back to the stable. See you folks around." Soon his truck was pulling the horse carrier down the driveway.

She looked at Wade. "Why? You didn't owe me this."

His expression defied description. "Maybe not, but maybe I did. It doesn't matter. I only know I love you, even if you never want to see me again. I fell in love with you the day you stormed into my office. You know, the night I was shot?"

He loved her? Had she heard that right? Stunned, all she could say was, "Of course I remember the night you were shot."

"I was on my way to your house."

"To my house? Why?"

"To talk. When you came into my office that afternoon, it brought back sweet memories."

"What memories? You didn't know I was alive. We never dated or spoke two words to each other."

"No, but I saw you riding in a horse show in Traverse City once. You were so beautiful, and you stole my heart that day. When you came into my office, I asked myself, what am I doing? There is the woman I admire—if I can win her."

"Why didn't you say something then?"

He laughed. "Being shot drove many things from my mind. Except an undeniable urge to reach out to you kept pushing me. Thank heaven Buck found me."

"Thank heaven I had to find Noona. But I meant back in high school."

"You were in ninth grade. I was a senior. You were too young. Then events transpired and time passed. We both followed different roads. Now we're back on the same path. I want to continue seeing you. Actually, I pretty much like being in your kitchen, but I can think of a few other places I'd like to be."

"I think I want to see you again, too. But why bring the horses back here? There is no one to keep an eye on them. Tina can't be here all the time."

"Well, I think the initial danger is past. Plus, I'm going to guarantee your land stays in your family. As part of my family, I hope. Will you marry me?"

He stood there, holding a colt so her daughter could safely pet the animal while he proposed to her. She let Noona go and took a step toward him. "We hardly know each other."

"Nonsense. I'll court you until you're sure if that's what you want. But we'll be married in May."

"That sounds like a cock-sure statement." She took another step toward him.

"You should marry him, Mommy. I like him."

"You like him?" she asked Kari as she took a step closer to Wade.

Close enough that Wade could put an arm around her waist. He kissed her forehead.

"Yes, I do. And he likes me, too."

Amanda looked at Wade. "This feels like a conspiracy. May's too soon. August." She placed a hand on his chest to push him back far enough to see his face.

"June." His head bent to hers, their foreheads touched.

She smiled a breath away from his lips. "How about July?" Amanda kissed him.

"That's a yes?" Wade said after a long interlude. She nodded. "Good. Now I can show you my engagement gift for you."

"What?"

"Come to my truck. Come on, Kari." Once the paddock gate closed, he pulled her by the hand, Kari taking his other hand. At his new truck, he pulled out a long tube and handed it to Amanda with a broad smile and gleaming eyes.

She opened the tube and pulled out a roll of papers. Unrolling the papers, she looked at a house plan. "But this is...was, my house!" The interior floor plan remained nearly the same. The outside elevations were exactly the way the stone shell in the yard looked before the fire.

"I've been working on them since the fire, but I didn't want to show you until I knew you would accept me without thinking I was asking you to marry me because you saved my life. The plan's almost the same, but with a few small improvements."

"Let me see," Kari said. Wade lifted her to stand in the truck's bed.

"A few small improvements?" Amanda asked in a faint voice.

He moved behind her, his body sheltering hers as his finger traveled over the prints as he talked. "The outside remains essentially the same. I've already had an engineer inspect the walls, and he thinks they will be approved for rebuilding. If not, we'll have them reinforced so it won't be noticeable. We'll take and expand the back so we can enlarge the kitchen, modernize the bathroom and add on an upstairs retreat. Taking down the two stone walls inside the house will provide stone for the project." He rambled on about the changes, but Amanda became lost in her thoughts. *Her house. Their house, if she wanted. He was doing this for her, but he wanted it for them. So did she.*

All her fear melted away.

She looked up at him through blurry vision. "You're sure this isn't because of any misplaced sense of obligation?"

Wade put his arms around her waist. It felt like coming home.

"For saving my life? No. You said yourself, Buck saved me."

Amanda's giggle was broken as she sniffed her runny nose. "Yes, he did."

"I love you. I have since you were in ninth grade but forgot until you rushed back into my life. The feeling only grows. I love your daughter and want to make her mine. I want to live with you in a fine stone farmhouse where we can raise horses, dogs, apples, and children. Please..."

She felt tears line her eyes. "I loved you in high school but knew my attraction was doomed. You were too popular and graduated ahead of me. Then life and circumstances happened, bringing you back, plus while you lay bleeding on my kitchen floor, I knew what I felt was doomed again." She rolled up the house plan and inserted it back in the cardboard roll, giving it to Kari, who hugged it. Placing a hand on his chest, she saw his doubt. "I've come to love you, too, but was doubtful, and after Grant, I will admit to not trusting any man. While your promises about the orchard, the stone house rebuild, and giving me Noon and her foal back are wonderful inducements, it was when you showed your love for Kari, and even Buck, that you convinced me. Yes, I want to marry you." She kissed him.

Meet Rhobin Courtright

Born and raised in Michigan, Rhobin spent one year in Colorado and twenty years in Missouri raising her family and working as a business writer. She now lives back in Michigan on twenty acres of forest near the small village of Luther. Always interested in science, history, nature, and art, her overactive imagination led her to speculate on life beyond Earth, and the 'what-ifs' of changes to humanity that soon turned into fantasy and science fiction novels. She writes about writing and her quirks of mind here: www.rhobincourtright.com

Other Works From The Pen Of Rhobin Courtright

Aegis Series:

Magic Aegis - Centuries ago, the witch Chloe cast the Aegis spell, binding four men and their descendants to protect Kaereya. Now, when needed most, magic is lost.

Change - Her mother demanded two things of Tyna: that she never expose her true nature and that she never enter Cygna, the land of witches. Now, her mother is dead and her sister has abandoned her.

Acceptance - Responsibility and duty drive mercenary Kissre to find her estranged sister in Cygna, the land of witches.

Legend's Cipher - What Bertok had not related when the bishop gave him this mission was his most buried secret—he possessed an unnatural ability.

Black Angel Series:

Rogue's Rules - Traitor, mutineer, deserter—slanderous words fixed to Ensign Jezlynn Chamber's name.

Loser's Game - Jezlynn has plied the pirates' trade but won't let anyone use the signature of the Black Angel to hide their crimes.

Devil's Due - Command ordered Jezlynn into the Space Service Corp, yet it is one thing to think you can accomplish a goal, another to achieve it.

Angels Tread – Just when Jezlynn believes she has overcome her past, it returns to haunt her.

Home World Series:

Home World Aginfeld - On technically advanced but feudal Aginfeld, Alix Risseu is held for theft...the sentence is death. Only Alix is innocent.

Nanite Warrior - Hearing herself claimed as wife, Xandra gave a weak laugh. "Bad luck just won't end, but this time, I'm sure yours is worse than mine, husband.

Dragoons' Journey - Brigit has moved constantly for years, now a message offers her freedom on Aginfeld, a place her enemy, the Colonial Pact, desperately wants.

Home World Reax - Maera escaped the future planned for her on Reax, so what could make her return? Learning of her home planet's devastation.

The Carolingians:

Constantine's Legacy – Leonard must learn to be the Frankish warrior his father, Radulf the Dux Provinciae demands. His difficult training is nothing compared to the dangerous deceptions he discovers.

Letter to Our Readers

Enjoy this book?

You can make a difference

As an independent publisher, Wings ePress, Inc. does not have the financial clout of the large New York Publishers. We can't afford large magazine spreads or subway posters to tell people about our quality books.

But, we do have something much more effective and powerful than ads. We have a large base of loyal readers.

Honest Reviews help bring the attention of new readers to our books.

If you enjoyed this book, we would appreciate it if you would spend a few minutes posting a review on the site where you purchased this book or on the Wings ePress, Inc. webpages at:
https://wingsepress.com/